Red Zone

Rangers Football

Book 5

Kameron Claire

Snuggle Whore Press, LLC

Contains explicit love scenes and adult language. The suggested reading audience is 18 years or older.

Covers by SWP Covers

To all the Witty, Wicked & Wild Readers...
Never let them silence our Witty tongues,
Never let them shame our Wicked needs,
Never let them stop our Wild deeds.

Thank you for the love and support!

ROCKY MOUNTAIN
RANGERS

Prologue

"I say we invite that one and that one and, of course, the redhead over there back to our hotel."

Rex shakes his head. "Coach will have our ass if he finds out we bought a bunch of strippers home with us."

"Dancers—" Jepson flashes a brunette his Sunday school smile "—and the coach isn't invited."

"Dancers, whatever," Rex rolls his eyes

"Which one do you like, Jaxson?"

Jaxson shrugs and tosses back what's left of his beer. "I don't care."

"Sure you do. You want the redhead, don't you?" Jepson taunts. "He always goes for the redhead."

Jaxson rolls his eyes. "Actually, I was digging the blonde."

"I already called dibs on the blonde," Jepson smirks, his eye contact hard across the table at his brother.

"Of course, you did," Jaxson mutters.

The blonde in question comes up and flashes the table a big smile. "Anyone looking for a lap dance?"

"Actually, honey, we were hoping for something a bit more intimate," Jepson leans forward.

She tsks and throws him a placating smile. "I'm sure you are, but this is not that kind of establishment."

"I'm sure for the right price it could be any kind of establishment we want."

"Where are you boys from?"

"Spring City, Colorado. What about you?"

"I'm Nashville, born and raised, sugar."

Jepson lets his eyes trail down her body. "What time do you get off work?"

"Why?" She straightens, putting more distance between her and him.

"The boys would love to see Music Row. Since you are homegrown, you could show us all the places only the locals go."

"Every place on Music Row is good and they are easy to find. Just walk a straight line and follow your nose or your ears, depending upon what you are looking for."

"But don't you want to entertain a couple of big badass football players?"

Plastering on a sweet smile, she bats her eyelashes. "My boyfriend is a big badass football player."

"From Nashville?" Rex arches his brow.

"You damn right," she replies.

"Yeah, but Nashville sucks," Jepson chuckles. "We're going to be National champions this year, honey.

Wouldn't you like to suck the dick of a winner at least once this year?"

Her smile fades, and she turns to walk away. Jepson reaches out and grabs her hand—the one thing you're not allowed to do.

"Man, don't touch the dancers," Rylie says, putting his drink down. He looks over his shoulder at security, which is walking their way. "We're not in Denver and the women here don't know you like that, so keep your hands to yourself."

"Fuck you, choirboy," Jepson releases her hand and puts his hands in his lap. "Sorry honey. I didn't mean to infer you'll be sucking my dick. It could be one of my teammates."

She looks over our heads and shakes her head, letting the security guard know it's okay for the moment. "You're an asshole."

Jepson smiles. "Yeah, but I'm a hot asshole."

She rolls her eyes and walks away. At the same time, a waitress walks up with another round of drinks. We are not supposed to be drinking tonight and yet Jepson's on his third whiskey on the rocks. His twin brother Jaxson is nursing his beer and Devlin, Rylie, and Rex are drinking Diet Coke.

"We should get out of here and check out a couple of local artists on our walk back to the hotel," Devlin says, throwing down a twenty and standing, brokering no questions that he's leaving. Rylie also stands, throwing down his own Jackson, and follows Devlin out.

Prologue Continued

Rylie

Devlin and I walk a couple of blocks down a side road back to Broadway. Music and people filter in and out of neon-lit buildings, the crowds thick on this warm and sticky Saturday night.

"Think they've been kicked out or arrested yet?" I ask Devlin.

"I hope not." He mutters. "We'd be in just as much trouble for leaving them behind."

"Does everyone think I come off as a choirboy?"

"No man. The difference between you and them is experience and responsibility. You have it, they don't. Don't let it bother you."

"How much time do we have?" My eyes lock onto a brightly lit tourist shop. Rarely do I have time during our travels to pick up anything outside of the airport gift shop knick-knacks, and Nyla will give me hell if I don't bring her something from music town, which is what my little girl calls Nashville. She loves music and wants to come here someday. Maybe I'll take her to Dollywood after the season is over.

"A little over an hour until curfew." Devlin looks above the tourist shop at the bar with excellent guitar riffs floating down from the rooftop.

"I'm going to find Nyla a gift."

Devlin nods. "I'll be upstairs for a couple of songs if you want to meet me. If not, I'll see you in the morning."

I enter the bustling shop and work my way toward the corner of merchandise that caters to children. My daughter has an interesting sense of style—a perfect combination of tomboy and princess. Her favorite Sunday outfit is her football jersey coupled with a color coordinated tutu and glitter rain boots. She says it's my lucky outfit, and she has to wear it to keep me safe.

I'm checking out a straw hat with a rainbow band wrapped around the brim when my phone rings. Checking the screen, a ball drops in my gut.

"Hey, Gloria." I try to sound chipper with my ex-mother-in-law. We have a great relationship, but if she's calling me on a Saturday night, something is wrong. "Everything okay?"

"Hi, Rylie. Can you talk?"

"To you? Always."

She sighs. "We have Nyla with us."

Any hope I had that this conversation would be anything different from what I expected dies instantly. "Where is Heather?"

"Gone. She dropped off Nyla a couple of hours ago. We weren't going to tell you until after the game tomorrow, but Sam's having trouble catching his breath, so we're at the hospital."

"What's going on?" I put down my items and walk out of the noisy store in search of a quieter space. "Are you okay? Do you need me to come home?"

Although Gloria and Sam are my ex-in-laws and Nyla's grandparents, I care for them. Their daughter, my ex-wife, is a shit show, but they are good to my child, so I make sure they get the time they want with Nyla.

"Right now, they are performing tests to make sure he doesn't have a blocked artery or something critical. I have Nyla here with me. She's playing in a children's room."

I sigh. "I'll catch the next flight back."

"No, Rylie. Nyla is keeping me company right now, and honestly, I need her here with me. The reason I'm calling is—" I hear Gloria choke back a sob "—it's time for you to stop being the nice guy. You need to petition the court for full custody of Nyla to protect her from Heather. It kills me to say this about my daughter, but she doesn't deserve access to this little girl."

I nod, not giving her verbal confirmation. Once we filed for divorce, I had hoped Heather would get her partying out of her system during the week and pull her shit together for her weekends with Nyla. She gets every weekend I'm out of town for games, and then a week during the summer, not that we've gotten that far yet. It's only been a year, but this isn't the first time she's dumped our daughter on her parents. "I'll text my lawyer tonight and start the paperwork on Monday."

"And..." Gloria hedges. "You should get a live-in

nanny. We love Nyla and want to spend as much time as possible with her, but we're too old to take on a four-year-old in the middle of the night."

I sigh again. This has been a thought bouncing around in my head, but I hate admitting my utter failure as a parent by bringing on someone full-time. At this point, it's my only way to protect Nyla, provide her stability, and do my job on the field. Where the fuck does someone find a reputable live-in nanny? "I understand. I'm sorry."

"You have nothing to be sorry for, son. I'm sorry about Heather. I wish I could explain her, but honestly, I can't. Someday she's going to look back on her life and realize she threw away the best thing that ever happened to her."

"I'm not sure what to say to that, Gloria."

"I guess there isn't anything to say, Rylie. Do you want to talk to Nyla?"

"Yes, please."

"One minute."

I listen as Gloria opens a door. I know this because a cartoon playing in the background grows louder. "Daddy's on the phone."

My little girl's voice comes on the line, happy as always. "Hi, Daddy."

"Hey, Princess. Are you being good for Nammy and Pappa?"

"Yes."

"Are you scared at the hospital?"

"No. Nammy says we can have pancakes tomorrow."

Chuckling, I lean my back against the side of the brick building and cross my legs at my ankles. "Sounds yummy. What did your momma tell you before she dropped you off at Nammy's house?"

Nyla sighs and I can imagine her rolling her eyes. "She has to work."

I shake my head. God only knows what that means. Boyfriends? Parties? Is she working the pole again or worse to get her fix?

"Did you buy me a present?" My little girl pipes up with her one-track mind.

"I'm at the store right now."

"Will you buy me a cowboy hat?"

"Maybe." We're incredibly in sync. Or maybe she's told me a million times she wants a cowboy hat to match her game-day apparel, but it has to be from a place where cowboys roam free. We live in Colorado where there are a ton of ranches, but the only suitable cowboy places in her mind are Nashville, Texas, and maybe Montana.

"Please, Daddy!"

"Be good for Nammy and Pappa and I'll see what I can do. Okay?"

"Okay. You're home tomorrow, right?"

"Yes, ma'am. I should be home in time for dinner."

"Can we get McDonald's?"

I curl my lips in disgust. "I was thinking Red Robin, if I get home early enough." She loves their strawberry lemonade, which has way too much sugar for her at six o'clock at night, but I know she'll pick it over Mickey Ds, any day.

"Yay!"

"All right, Princess. I got to go. Give the phone back to Nammy, okay?"

"Love you, Daddy."

"I love you more."

Gloria gets back on the phone. "Hi again, Rylie."

"If you need me, I'll board the first flight home."

"I know you will. Sammy is on his way and will help us this evening if need be. Have a good game tomorrow, and let us know when you are on your way."

"I will. Thank you, Gloria, for everything."

"Nyla is my grand-baby. I will always be there for her... and you."

Shit. Now I have to hire a live-in nanny.

Chapter 1

Rylie

"I need to grab my phone out of my locker. When is Coach going to loosen the reins?" I mumble to Rex, sitting to my left.

He shakes his head slowly. "I don't know, but the tension around the team is unbearable."

I catch Gar's eye, one of the defensive coordinators, and throw him a pleading look. He glances at the coach and then motions to the side of the room. As quietly as possible, I maneuver through rows of tired, frustrated, and tense men.

"What's up?"

"I need to check my phone. My daughter calls every day to let me know she's home from school and, according to my watch, she hasn't called yet."

As a new parent himself, he nods and motions to the door. "Go. I'll take care of it."

Slipping out of the room, I walk-jog to the lockers, glancing once again at my smartwatch. Normally she texts and I can respond with a pre-programmed note, letting her know I love her and will see her soon. Sending me a note is the highlight of her day, so to have her two hours late causes me serious distress.

She's only four years and eleven months—as she likes to remind me daily—so I haven't burdened her with a phone to carry on her body yet, although I will admit to being the guy who put GPS trackers in her shoes and on her backpack. Of course, she's lost both, and the day she traded shoes with a boy in class almost gave me a heart attack.

I call Brenda, the pseudo-live-in nanny I hired three months ago. I say pseudo, because she's more of an overnight babysitter on the nights I'm out of town, but otherwise she doesn't stay in the house when I'm home. Her boyfriend refused that arrangement and I settled for what I can get right now.

Nyla likes her well enough, but something tells me I'm going to be looking for a new nanny sooner rather than later.

The call to Brenda goes straight to voicemail, ratcheting up my anxiety a few notches. I bring up the GPS app to see Nyla's backpack and shoes still at her school, a full two hours after she should have been home.

What the fuck?

I grab my wallet and keys and am running down the corridor toward the garage before I can think twice about it. Jumping into my Jeep, I dial the school over the car's audio system. At the same time, an unknown number hits my phone. It's only now that I realize I've missed three calls from this number.

"Hello?" I half bark.

"Mr. Reynolds?" A soft voice asks warily.

"This is he."

"My name is Sunshine Mitchell. I'm a teacher's aide for Nyla's class."

"Is she okay?"

"She's fine. We're sitting here drawing pictures for each other. Her caretaker didn't show up today and we haven't been able to get in touch with anyone."

"I'm on my way right now," I say as I pull into traffic. "I should be there in fifteen minutes."

"Okay. We'll meet you in front of the school."

"Why didn't the school call the emergency number? The administration would've pulled me off the field if there was an emergency."

"Well..." The sweet, lyrical voice on the other end hedges, "The school is pretty intolerant about no-shows, and I didn't want to make a big deal about this until it was one. She's safe at the school with me, and it's not even five o'clock yet, so I told them we had prearranged a late pickup. I figured I would get them involved after five if I couldn't get in touch with you or Brenda. Otherwise, they'd make your life hell. I know, I've seen them do it to other parents."

I sigh, annoyance warring with gratitude. "Can I talk to Nyla?"

"Sure." The woman's voice gets bright as she hands over the phone.

"Hi, Daddy."

"Hey, Princess. You okay?"

"Yep. We're drawing pictures. Miss Sunshine is an amazing artist."

"You can show me when I get there. I'm on my way. I love you."

"Love you too." My little girl hangs up without another word.

Where the fuck is Brenda? Yes, she's less focused on my daughter than I would like, but I didn't think she was irresponsible, and I in no way thought she would be cavalier about Nyla's safety.

I call Brenda one more time, and when it goes straight to voicemail, I call the nanny service. Gritting my teeth, I wait for the voicemail recording to finish so I can leave a message. "This is Rylie Reynolds. My nanny, Brenda Days, isn't picking up her phone and neglected to pick up my daughter from school today. I need someone to call me immediately."

Hanging up, a thought flitters through my brain. What if she was in an accident, is in the hospital, or worse? That quells my anger a bit. I know she stays with her boyfriend on the nights I'm in town, but otherwise, I don't know a lot about her. Twenty-three, she was working in a nursing home before signing on with the service. I'm her first client.

My phone beeps as I pull into the parking lot with an incoming message, my car reading the text to me in its mechanical voice.

"Sorry, Mr. Reynolds. My boyfriend proposed to me

today and we're celebrating. He says I'm not allowed to work for a single man anymore, so consider this my notice."

Rage colors my vision as I roll to a stop in front of the school, blinding me from seeing the woman sitting with Nyla. I step out of my Jeep in a haze until I focus on my daughter with her blonde curls and big, toothless smile.

"Daddy! Look at my picture." She thrusts a crayon masterpiece that rivals Picasso into my hands.

Nyla is safe, and that's all that matters right now. My little girl is more mature than she should have to be as an almost five-year-old, and untethered enthusiasm from her is rare, so I feel an overwhelming wave of gratitude for her energy. I swoop her up into my arms and clutch her to my chest. "It's amazing, Princess."

"Hi." That soft, melodic voice from earlier pulls my focus and my eyes settle on a gorgeous redhead with soft brown eyes. "I'm Sunshine."

"Sunshine?"

She giggles as we shake hands. "Yeah, my parents were hippies, or at least that's what I tell everyone."

"That's your real name?"

"Uh, yes."

I nod. "I'm forever in your debt, Sunshine. Brenda just called and gave her notice, effective immediately."

"No more Brenda, Daddy?"

"No. I guess not."

"Good," Nyla says without emotion.

"Good? Why do you say that? Is there something you need to tell me?"

She shakes her curls, motioning for me to let her down.

I set her on her feet and grab her bag from the bench.

"No, nothing bad. But she never wanted to play. If she wasn't talking or texting on her phone, she was creating Pinterest boards of her perfect wedding. And then the few times I met her boyfriend, I didn't like him. He reminds me of the guys' momma hangs out with."

I clench my jaw to stop the profanities from flying off my tongue. If he reminds her of those dirtbags, he's not a nice guy and someone I didn't want around my child. "Was he at the house?"

"Sometimes in the driveway, but never inside."

Nodding my head, I open the back door and throw in her bag. "Are you hungry?"

"Miss Sunshine shared her snack with me, but I'm still hungry." Nyla climbs in behind me. She's tall for her age, even though she's still in a booster seat.

"She did?" I glance at the redhead who is way too pretty to be a kindergarten teacher's aide. I bet all the kids adore her. Part of me wants to hug her for being a good person. Part of me knows that would be a bad idea judging by her lush curves softened by a fuzzy sweater with kittens on it.

Sunshine blushes. "It was just cheese and nuts and maybe a few M&M's."

"How will I ever repay you for your kindness?"

"Can Miss Sunshine come to dinner with us?" Nyla asks.

"I wasn't aware we were going to dinner..." I raise my

brow, challenging her blatant manipulation tactic. One thing my little girl loves to do is eat out. She has an impressive palate, way more diverse than my cooking skills can keep up with.

"Please, Daddy."

"Where are we going?" I'm going to give in. I always give in.

"What do you want, Miss Sunshine? Italian, Mexican, or sushi?"

"Sushi?" she giggles. "I don't know many four-year-olds who eat sushi."

Nyla corrects her. "I'll be five in a few weeks and I've been eating raw fish since I was three, right Daddy?"

"Uh, kind of." I turn to look at Sunshine, which might be the most ridiculous and yet appropriate name I've ever heard for a person. Her kindness shines off her, radiates from within, and I could see how she's a ray of sunshine for the people in her life. "She's been eating California rolls and sushi bakes since three. We only introduced salmon and tuna a couple of weeks ago."

"Still, it's impressive."

"Would you like to go to dinner with us? It's the least I can do."

She bites her lip and looks back at the school. "I'm not supposed to fraternize with the students or their parents outside of the classroom."

I nod. "I understand."

"But I adore Nyla, and she did eat most of my snack." Sunshine grins. "Can I follow you in my car?"

A pair of adorable dimples pop in her cheeks and I

swear something inside me sparks to life. "I'll drive slow."

"Okay." She waves at Nyla and whispers in an almost conspiratorial tone, "I'll see you soon."

Climbing behind the steering wheel, I glance back at my little girl, who has finished fastening all of her belts. "So, that's the infamous Miss Sunshine?" Nyla has been talking about her for the last couple of months.

"Yep. I really like her. She's nice to everyone, but firm and fair when she has to be. Like, she doesn't let Misty tease anyone, and she doesn't let Johnny push others around. Everyone loves her."

"I'm sorry about Brenda. I wish you had told me earlier."

"You have enough on your plate, Daddy. I could handle Miss Brenda."

I take in a deep breath and let it out slowly. My little girl is so mature for her age. She's a blessing, and yet I wonder if these early experiences will adversely affect her teenage years. Yes, maybe I have more than enough on my plate, but she is the only thing that matters. I'll give it all up if I need to. But that's way too heavy of a conversation to have with an almost five-year-old. "Where to, boss?"

She giggles. Nyla loves it when I call her boss. "I think Miss Sunshine needs sushi."

"Okay then."

I send a text to Gar to let him know what happened and that I'll pay the penance tomorrow. He replies with a thumbs-up emoji. Thankfully, the Rangers are a family-focused organization, so I suspect the backlash to my slipping out early will be minimal. We've been on lockdown for over a month—ever since a handful of public embarrassments pissed the coaches and GM off enough to put us under a curfew as if we are a bunch of college students —but honestly, mostly it doesn't affect me.

My life is football and Nyla—and she enjoys nights at home falling asleep to a movie.

I don't date. One, because I don't have the time and two, I don't have the energy. After Heather, I don't know if I'll ever have the energy again.

Do I miss sex? Yes, but my hand does a fine job with none of the drama my ex-wife brought into my world. Besides, I can't risk bringing anyone into Nyla's life that isn't one hundred percent about my daughter, and it's ridiculous to think I will meet and date a woman who feels that way about my child from the get-go.

So why even go there?

We pull into the parking lot while an older model Nissan Sentra parks next to us.

I'm already going through the Rolodex of players' wives I might hit up for babysitting over the weekend. We play at home this Sunday, so I need someone willing to let Nyla play with their kids while we are on the field. I try not to abuse the same wives over and over again, considering I can't repay them with babysitting during the season. Next summer, I'm sure I'll be hosting a houseful of kids for a couple of weeks straight, but until then, my career makes being a single father damn near impossible.

I wonder if Sunshine babysits?

Nyla skips ahead of us to the door, pulling Sunshine forward. "Have you been here before?"

Sunshine chuckles. "No. Is it good?"

"It's so cool. Right, Daddy?"

I shrug. "They have a conveyor belt system, which Nyla finds fascinating."

"That does sound fascinating." Sunshine nods and smiles down at my daughter before sending a wink my way. There's something about the effortless way she is with Nyla and me that puts me at ease immediately, as if we've known each other for a lifetime.

We sit at the bar, a conveyor belt with brightly colored plates traveling past us. The system is simple. Grab what you want, stack your used plates, and they charge you at the end. Luckily, Nyla can't reach the plates on her own, which means, for the moment, I still have some semblance of control. Sunshine picks up the routine quickly, and before I know it, we're happily eating.

"So, Sunshine, tell me about yourself."

Her eyes grow wide as she covers her mouth to finish chewing on a piece of norimaki. "There's not much to tell. I graduated from DU last May and this is my first job as a teacher's aide."

"Did you move to town for this job, or is this where you are from?"

"I moved here for it. Originally, I'm from Kansas, but I love Colorado and couldn't afford Denver. Heck, I can barely afford to live in Spring City with a roommate."

"I see." I chew on my piece of sashimi, giving Nyla a

half piece of salmon. "What time do you normally get off work? I mean, how long did you have to stay after to keep Nyla company?"

She wrinkles her nose and shakes her head. "Trust me. I was looking for a reason to not go home tonight anyway, so staying late was a blessing."

"Why do you not want to go home?" I stare at her face—smooth skin with light freckles over the bridge of her nose and cheeks lead me to believe her red hair is natural. She's got plump, kissable lips that turn up the barest amount in the corners, giving her an almost permanent impish grin. Her teeth appear to be straight except for the top front, which is slightly turned inward. She's got the disposition of her name, but her curves are built for sin, which she downplays with oversized, kid-friendly attire. Given she's teaching kindergarten, I'd say downplaying her figure is the right move.

Still—any man can see through the fuzzy kitties to the body underneath and lust after it.

She sighs and casts a furtive glance at Nyla. "My roommate has a new friend who I used to know. He likes to come over and read her stories loudly, as if he's putting on a show. Right now he's reading Jack and the Bean *Stalk*."

I furrow my brow. What is she talking about?

Nyla also looks up with a curious look on her little face.

"If you're trying to speak around a subject for Nyla's benefit, it won't work. My little girl is wicked smart and I find it easier to speak plainly."

Sunshine smiles down at Nyla. "I'm sorry, sweetie. I wasn't trying to exclude you, but I didn't want to tell a story that upset you."

Nyla nods and returns to her sushi.

Sunshine continues. "I moved here in mid-June and found my roommate online renting out a furnished room. This guy—ironically his name is Jack—we dated for a couple of weeks before I graduated college up in Denver. I told him from the beginning it wasn't serious because I knew I would move away. Well, I think he followed me here late this summer because a few weeks ago he started dating my roommate. I know, because after hearing her and her new boyfriend *read all night*, I opened my door in the morning and found him standing in the hallway outside of my room. He hasn't come out and said it, but I feel like he's stalking me."

I stare at her, a protective need rising in my chest. Unfortunately, jumping into her problems exposes my little girl, which is the last thing I'm willing to do.

"She could take over Brenda's room," Nyla says out of nowhere.

"What?" I damn near choke on my green tea.

"Well, she doesn't want to go home to her bed, and Brenda isn't sleeping in hers anymore, so why can't Miss Sunshine take over that room?"

I have wondered if she would be interested in a nanny position, but now I have to be worried about what kind of baggage she brings with her.

Still, it's not a half-bad idea.

Chapter 2
Sunshine

I can't believe I vented my problems to my student and her *way-too-hot-to-be-real* father. Nyla spent the last two hours telling me everything about her life, which includes a mother who doesn't want to be a mommy, and a perfect daddy who plays football for the Rocky Mountain Rangers. Brenda, her nanny, isn't any fun, and she would much rather spend her time with me, even if it is at school.

I have to admit, Nyla is the perfect little girl because she's not only inquisitive and creative, but she's also outspoken, courageous, and will always be the first one to stand up for other little girls and boys. She has a good sense of right or wrong instilled in her, and I know that comes from the man sitting to my left.

Rylie Reynolds is beyond gorgeous. He's tall and wide, and I can't keep my eyes from drifting down to his big hands that, in any other situation, I would fantasize about roaming all over me. Yes, I have a thing about large hands and what they'd look like sliding up my curves. I'm not exactly an exhibitionist, but I love the art of burlesque and erotic photography.

Someday, when I meet the right man, we'll get sexy photos done together.

Add to his large and imposing presence, Rylie has dark hair—a complete contrast to Nyla's light blonde curls—piercing blue eyes, and a strong jawline with hollowed cheeks, which gives him a rugged look. I bet he would photograph beautifully.

Ugh, I should not be having thoughts like this—but how can I not when he looks so good?

"Are you in danger with this man lurking in your apartment?" Rylie's face is a mask of seriousness.

I shake my head. "He has said nothing that makes me think I'm in danger, but I lock my door at night. Otherwise, I don't think I would get a minute of sleep. My roommate doesn't care that he's my ex, and she believes he's there solely for her. I hope she's right, but meanwhile, I'm trying to find another place to live. I wish I could afford to live by myself, but there's no way on my teacher's aide salary."

"You don't have friends you can stay with?"

"Well, I moved here this summer, but I haven't made any friends yet. I'll be okay—" I wink at Nyla "—I always have a way of landing on my feet."

"Have you ever been a nanny before?" Rylie asks casually.

I shrug. "I mean, I take care of kids all day and babysat when I was a kid. What else does the job entail other than taking care of what needs to be taken care of in the home?"

Rylie stares down at his plate, contemplating his words. "Brenda quit on me today with no notice, so not only do I have an empty room at my house, but I'm in desperate need of someone I can trust with Nyla. She seems to trust you implicitly, so maybe I can, too?"

Nyla clasps her hands together and hops in her seat. "Yes! You can come live with us and we'll have pancakes on Saturday, watch cartoons, draw, and then play on my swing set outside..."

Oh my goodness. She is so sweet, but unfortunately, this is an offer I don't think I can take—at least not permanently. "I'm pretty sure it's against school policy for me to be a live-in nanny for one of my students, but maybe we can come to a temporary arrangement where we keep it as our little secret?" I purposely look at Nyla.

She nods. "I can keep a secret."

Rylie narrows his eyes. "I'm not a fan of secrets, but what did you have in mind?"

"It sounds like you need someone immediately and it will take a few days to weeks to vet another full-time nanny. I could use that time to find another place to live while taking care of Nyla. As long as we keep it on the down-low, I think we could work something out."

"Can you come by the house tonight?"

"I already have a bag packed in my car." Chucking, I turn my gaze to the conveyor belt and snag a couple of pieces of a complex roll with salmon, tuna, and masago. I haven't slept a full night in weeks and was planning on staying at a hotel tonight, but this is even better.

Rylie takes a deep breath and then rolls his shoulders, visibly relaxing for the first time since we met an hour ago.

Twenty minutes later, I'm following them into a nice gated neighborhood. There are row upon row of large houses, but not what I would call mansions. Definitely in the three-quarter of a million range, but not so over the top that the neighborhood feels pretentious. Some driveways have gates in front of them, while others—Rylie's in particular—do not. Two garage doors open, but I wait in the driveway as Rylie pulls into the one on the right. He jumps out and points to the open door next to him, inviting me in to park my dilapidated Nissan in the garage.

Of course, my first thought is that I hope I'm not dripping oil on his pristine concrete floors. That would be embarrassing.

"I'll get you a garage door opener and a key fob for the community gate. As long as you're coming in and out through the garage, we'll input your code to the door. I can do that tonight while I'm zeroing out all of Brenda's access."

"This is a lot more convenient than trying to gather keys from people."

"Yeah. Thank god for the digital age."

I grab my bag out of the backseat and follow them into the house. Nyla is jumping around, excited to be in charge of the tour. Rylie chuckles, shakes his head, and motions for me to follow her. "This will be your room. Daddy and I sleep on the second floor, so you would have this area to yourself."

She ushers me into a bedroom that has its own bathroom. It's twice the size of my current living situation. It even has a sliding glass door that goes out onto a tiny patio of its own on the side of the house. "Nice."

"You'll like living with us. Do you want to see my playroom?"

"Of course I do."

Nyla takes me downstairs into a basement that is a half playroom and half workout facility. It has a pair of sliding glass doors that lead out to a patio covered by the deck from upstairs. In the yard is an impressive jungle gym.

"Something tells me you're a little spoiled." I grin down at the little girl, who responds by putting her hands on her hips.

"Uh uh. I'm not spoiled. I'm the princess."

I chuckle. "You certainly are."

Rylie comes down the stairs behind us with his phone in his hand. "What's your number? Is it the one you called from earlier?"

Any other situation and a man who looks like Rylie asking for my phone number would send my heart racing. Unfortunately, this is business.

Just my luck.

"Yes." I prattle off my number again when my phone pings in my purse.

"That was from me. I'm going to use the last four of

your phone number as your code to the house and alarm system." He studiously focuses on his phone, opening apps and changing access, his mind singularly focused.

"Okay." Nyla and I exchange a look and giggle at his furrowed brow.

He lifts his eyes to meet mine. "What?"

"You look so serious."

Sighing, he hits a couple more buttons and then closes out the apps before sliding his phone into his pocket. "I think the reality of what Brenda did hit me just now. If you hadn't been willing to stay late with Nyla..." He shakes his head.

I reach out and wrap my fingers around his muscular forearm. "It's okay. Everything worked out perfectly. Do you believe in fate?"

His eyes narrow, and a sly grin spreads across his soft lips. "No."

I shrug and return his knowing grin. He wants to tease me, which I would let him do. With a name like Sunshine and my woo-woo beliefs about cosmic energy and the universe, I'm used to it. In some ways, I encourage it. I always know when things are going to work out, when to stress, and when to let nature run its course. It's worked out for me so far. "Well, I do. I also believe in a child's intuition. Nyla had a sense something was wrong all day, and she knew to come directly to me when Brenda didn't show up."

Nyla hugs her father's legs. "It's okay, Daddy. I'm safe."

He shakes his head and picks her up. "Well, despite

our crazy day, it's still a school night, and it's almost seven. Time to wind down. Should we take Miss Sunshine through our nightly routine?"

"Yes." Nyla nods sagely.

The nightly schedule is this: home and playtime are between three and six. Dinner is no later than six. Seven is quiet time to include a bath, the brushing of teeth, watching a show, reading, and then bed by eight.

"That's a very structured routine."

Rylie shrugs. "I have to be at the field by seven am, so I'm up really early every day of the week. Right now, I'm not getting home until almost seven thirty each night, so I don't get a lot of time with Nyla before we crash out. To be honest, we often fall asleep in front of the TV, and at some point I carry her to her room."

"It has to be hard being a single father while playing football."

"I'm not going to pretend like it's easy."

"Well, Rylie, I'm here to help."

Nyla knows how to bathe herself, but she allows an adult to check the temperature of the water before we leave her to it.

"Yell if you need us, Princess," Rylie says as he nearly closes the door, leaving a sliver of open space. He motions to her bedroom. "I usually sit nearby while she bathes. When I'm not here, you can chill, but I'd appreciate you being within yelling distance, in case she needs you."

"Not a problem."

"Once we have her settled, we'll clean out your room. I have fresh sheets and towels and stuff, but I haven't gone into Brenda's room since she came on a few months ago, so I have no idea if it is trashed or not."

"Nyla took me for a tour, and it looks fine to me."

He nods. "Would you be offended if I ran a background check on you?"

I think for a second and then plastered a smile on my face. "No. The school ran one on me a couple of months ago to offer me the job, so I can't think of anything you would find that would make you uncomfortable leaving me with your daughter."

"No secrets to tell me before I run the report?"

"None that I can think of." I keep my voice bright, but honestly, I only have one secret, and the school never found out about it, so I don't see how he would. Besides, my debt is almost paid and therefore my secret life is almost over, so I see no reason to bring it up.

"Maybe I should run a background check on you?" I tease.

"You can do that." He nods.

I wave his comment away. "I can't afford a background check, so I'll google you instead."

He sighs. "You'll learn three things about me on the first page of Google. One, I temporarily paralyzed Deacon Scott over three years ago, rendering his career-ending injury, and I did not handle it well. Two, there was a lot of speculation in the sports world because he recruited me from the Mustangs to the Rangers this past spring. Most people think he should hate me, others think he's a saint, but between the two of us, we know what's up. And three, my ex-wife was arrested on a drug possession charge about a year ago."

"Oh, my." I bite my lip. "That sounds like a story."

"It's a conversation for another time."

Nyla comes out wrapped in a ducky terry-cloth robe. "All clean."

"Good job, Princess. Put on your PJs and then we'll pull out your outfit for tomorrow." Rylie stands up and leaves her room to give her... privacy? I'm not exactly sure. I follow him out and stand in the hallway, casting him a curious raise of my brow.

"She's very independent and has been since she was like three, but ever since I told her girls can't come into the locker room at the stadium because there are naked men in there, she has told me boys aren't allowed in her locker room when she's naked unless it's an emergency." He shrugs. "I have no problem respecting her boundaries as long as she asks me for help when she needs it, which she always does."

"Ready." She calls to us. We enter her room and I watch from the doorway as Rylie works with Nyla to pick out her clothes for tomorrow. Then he motions for her to climb into bed. She pats the edge of her mattress and tells me to join her while Rylie settles into the big chair in the room's corner.

She hands me a brush and a rubber band. "Will you braid my hair while I read?"

"You are going to read to us? This is a treat."

She nods solemnly. "We trade off."

Rylie leans back in his chair and closes his eyes while

Nyla reads and I brush and braid her hair. There is something so comforting about this moment as I stare at the larger-than-life man who resembles a giant teddy bear stuffed into the corner of the room. You know the one... the six-foot tall plushie you lay out on the living room floor and cuddle with while watching TV?

Yeah, that's the one.

Ten minutes later, Nyla is setting the book down and lying back, sliding deeper under the covers. Rylie opens his eyes, gets up without a sound, removes the book and pulls her blankets up, kissing her on the cheek. The entire moment is unbelievably sweet, and I swear my ovaries might implode from witnessing it firsthand.

He nods toward the door, and I precede him out of the room as he whispers, "Night, Princess."

"Night Daddy. Night Miss Sunshine." She murmurs.

We go downstairs and Rylie stops by the laundry room, grabbing a fresh set of sheets and towels. "Here we go."

The bedroom isn't trashed at all, but I already told him that. Actually, it barely looks lived in to me and still has a new paint smell. "I guess she didn't sleep here often?"

He shakes his head. "Only on the nights I was out of town. Her boyfriend, now fiancé, is a control freak and didn't want her sleeping in the same house as a single male. Speaking of which, no boyfriends in the house when I'm not here. I can't have someone thinking that they can make themselves at home here with Nyla."

I shake my head. "Absolutely not. One, I don't have a

boyfriend, so this is not a problem. And two, I wouldn't disrespect your home by bringing anyone else in here, boyfriend or not. Do you have any girlfriends you need to introduce me to? I don't want a jealous woman getting up in my face for being in her man's home."

He snorts. "No. I don't have the time or the energy for a girlfriend."

"Oh, that's too bad." The words slip out before I can think better of them.

"Is it?" He arches his brow.

I shrug. "Well, I mean... you're a good-looking guy. You've got a fabulous little girl, and although I've only spent a couple of hours with you, you seem cool."

He chuckles as he pulls off the comforter and strips the bed.

I clutch the new sheets to my chest. "I can do this, Rylie. Remember, you are helping me out just as much as I'm helping you. I'm sure you're tired after a full day of practice, so you should go relax."

He continues to strip the bed and toss all the old sheets and towels into a pile before he sighs. "Let me give you a tour of the kitchen, and then we'll test your codes. I'll admit, I'm up at five, so I'm usually in bed by nine."

"I'm also an early-to-bed, early-to-rise kind of girl, so this will work out perfectly."

I toss the clean sheets on the bed. Just as I think he's about to gather up the dirty sheets, he pulls me against his chest and wraps his arms around me. "Thank you. Dear god, thank you so much. I don't know what I'd do without you right now."

I'm stunned into temporary paralysis, and then I slide my arms around his waist and squeeze him back. There's nothing sexual about his touch. This is unadulterated gratitude radiating from his chest onto mine. I know happy sunshine when I feel it, and this is it. "I'm happy I could be here for you and Nyla."

He lets out a deep breath, his body relaxing under my fingers. Then he gives me another squeeze and wraps his big hands around my shoulders, stepping back and putting a good two feet of distance between us. "Let me show you where everything is and give you a rundown of my schedule."

He gathers up the dirty sheets and towels and dumps them in the laundry room before walking to the kitchen. I'm in awe of this man. A powerhouse of a male, he's sweet and sensitive—which is in complete contrast with his larger-than-life presence.

I'm more than happy to be here tonight. I downplayed my discomfort with my ex lurking outside my bedroom multiple times over the last couple of weeks, and I'm thrilled to be sleeping under this roof. Even though I technically don't know Rylie Reynolds, I feel a million times safer with him than I would have at a hotel tonight. This arrangement will be perfect for both of us, as long as Nyla doesn't let it slip at school.

And if I have to tamp down my fantasies about the hottest dad of the coolest kid in my class, I'll just do that.

Chapter 3

Rylie

Even though my alarm goes off at five every day, that doesn't make me a morning person. I start each day with a shower and then I drink a protein shake before I climb the stairs to wake up Nyla. Then I start breakfast, and if she's not in the kitchen by the time the eggs are done, I'm calling up to her again at five forty-five. We eat together and then I'm out the door a little after six thirty.

But this morning I take a longer shower, as my dreams from last night replay in technicolor. It's been a long time since my fantasies have been so specific.

Long, red hair.

Light, brown eyes.

Freckled cheeks.

Plump, kissable lips.

Full breasts.

Wide hips.

And a tight, round ass was center stage as I tossed and turned in bed last night.

I cannot lust after Nyla's new nanny, no matter how temporary she is. My need for a reliable caretaker has to outweigh the need building in my balls. I don't know if I've ever met somebody so sweet and tempting. She's a blessing on our household, but a curse to my control.

Usually, my shower is just long enough to wake me up, but this morning I'm lathering up my hands and stroking my cock, remembering the feel of her pressed against my chest with my arms wrapped around her. She fit me perfectly, and if I'd been so inclined, I could've rested my chin on the top of her head and held her for hours. And you know, I don't think she would mind. She didn't tense in my arms, nor did she pull away. Maybe she needs to be cared for as much as I need her to care for Nyla and, maybe, me.

I know it's wrong.

Goddammit, I know it's wrong, but I flex my hand and stroke my neglected cock harder, taking me from zero to coming in a matter of seconds. I've been fucking my hand for more than a year anyway, so I'm a pro at this point.

Gritting my teeth, I swallow down the groans threatening to escape my lips as I shoot my load against the tile wall.

Is this going to be my new morning ritual? Possibly.

Especially if I'm haunted night after night by dreams of sliding between her thick, muscular thighs.

Shaking off the vision and the water out of my hair, I wrap a towel around my waist and push through my morning routine. To my surprise, Sunshine is in the kitchen, fumbling with the coffeemaker.

"Good morning." My voice is hoarse as my gaze travels over her long muscular legs on display. She's wearing a baggy T-shirt and sleep shorts, and although I don't think she's trying to be sexy—she most definitely is.

"Good morning." She says in a sing-song voice, her back to me as she lifts on her toes to pull down a couple of coffee cups, her shirt and shorts riding up a little higher to expose more mouthwatering flesh.

My eyes lock on the tattoos on her upper thighs. "Tattoos?"

She bites her lips and casts me a coy smile as she turns to face me. "Yeah."

"What are they?"

She bunches the legs of her shorts and pulls them up to reveal rainbow ribbons wrapped about each thigh and tied into cute bows. They are up high enough on her legs that they would never show in a skirt. "Cute."

She shrugs. "Do you have any tattoos?"

"A couple."

Waggling her brows, she tosses me a teasing grin. "Want to show me?"

I chuckle and shake my head. The idea of removing clothing with her gives me a semi, and this is not the time or place. "Not this morning."

"Party pooper." She giggles. "How do you take your coffee?"

"Black."

"Of course, you do." She rummages through my

refrigerator. "I'll have to buy some creamer on the way home from school today. Is it okay if I take Nyla with me to the store?"

"As long as you have eyes on her, I'm fine with after-school errands. I trust your judgment." Last night, I ran one of those one-hundred-dollar background checks using her full name and driver's license number. Nothing surprising came back. As she said, she's from a little town in the middle of Kansas. She went to school at DU, graduated last May, and started working at Rudy Elementary in August. She has no student loans, which surprised me, and no car loan. One credit card with a minimum balance, and no criminal history. Not even a parking ticket.

Honestly, I'm looking for big red flags, like the ones I should have looked for with Heather before knocking her up and getting married. She had two misdemeanor drug charges on her record, as well as a dropped public indecency charge. When we met, she was working in a lingerie shop in downtown Denver during the day and bartending two nights a week at a little hotel bar. I met her my first weekend in town before I even had secured an apartment of my own. The Denver Mustangs put their new recruits up at a hotel for the first two weeks, giving us time to find a place to live. We started hot and heavy, and being a farm-raised boy out of Iowa, she was the most exciting woman I'd ever met.

I fell hard quickly.

Heather got pregnant almost immediately, although we didn't know the first few months. The amount of partying we did—me, a kid just out of college in the big city with a woman who knew all about life in the fast lane—is scary when I think about how she was carrying Nyla at the time. Thank god, as soon as we figured it out, all that stopped. I proposed, we got married, and bought a house—setting up for our family and future, one that I was excited to have. Heather turned it on a dime, taking excellent care of herself and our unborn child for the next seven months. For the first couple of years, I thought things were great. A little over two years ago, I learned how absolutely wrong I was. Being gone all the time, it was easy to lose track of what is happening at home. She hid it well, but once I pulled the thread, a slew of secrets and lies fell from her bag of tricks, and I knew there was no way to salvage our relationship.

What was worse—she had no interest in changing who she was for me or Nyla.

Although we've been divorced for over a year, I only filed for sole custody three months ago. Heather didn't bother showing up to court to contest it, so naturally, the judge granted it.

Honestly, I can't imagine not wanting to be with our little girl. She's the best thing to happen to me.

"Do you have your phone on you?" I pull mine out of my jogger pants and bring up the grocery service app I use.

"Sure." Sunshine dashes into her room and comes back out. "What am I looking up?"

I text her the app. "Install this and log in with the credentials I sent you."

While she does that, I pull out my protein powder and frozen fruits and vegetables, tossing them on the counter next to the blender. I make quick work of assembling my breakfast smoothie and have everything put away when she brings her head up with a beautiful smile.

Damn, that's a vision worth waking up to every morning.

"What can I make for you for breakfast?" Sunshine puts her phone down and opens the refrigerator again. "Any food allergies or restrictions I need to consider?"

I wrap my fingers around her wrist to garner her attention, even though deep down I know I shouldn't be touching her. It feels too good and too right and it would be too easy to give in to my baser needs, pull her close, and claim those pouty lips. "You don't have to take care of me. Keep Nyla safe and shuttle her to the places she has to be, and you'll be doing more than enough."

She drags her eyes up from my hand on her wrist up to my face and her expression does something to me. Those are bedroom eyes, as if she likes the vision of my hand on her. "I'll have to make Nyla and me dinner anyway, so I might as well make extra in case you're hungry when you get home. Speaking of which, am I packing her lunches?"

Unwillingly, I let go and take a step back, putting distance between us before I cross the line. "They keep us well fed via a cafeteria at the training facility, and I have Nyla enrolled in the lunch program at school, but if you want to pack snacks, I'm sure she would love it. Use the app you downloaded to order groceries and anything else you need for the house."

"I can pay for my food, Rylie."

"You won't while you are living here with us, Sunshine. Speaking of which, I was paying the nanny service weekly. Would you like me to direct deposit to your bank account or pay you via PayPal or Venmo or whatever while you're here?"

Sunshine rests her hips against the counter and frowns. "You're not paying me. We're helping each other out, remember?"

"I'm paying you. I was paying the service seven fifty a week, which includes room and board. They gave her insurance, which is the only thing I can't offer you."

Her jaw drops. "Brenda walked away from three thousand dollars a month for taking care of a little girl who practically takes care of herself? Jeez. Maybe I should come on full-time?"

My heart skips a beat. That would be perfect for Nyla and pure torture for me. "If you want to discuss it later, let me know."

"I wish." She frowns. "I'm sure there's a policy against it, although I need to look up the rules. I mean, some teachers have kids at the school, so maybe there are loopholes to exploit. Speaking of which—" she snaps her fingers "—you need to call the school and authorize me to take Nyla out of class, otherwise they won't let her leave with me."

"Okay. What should I tell them?"

"I'll let them know I'm house-sitting around the

corner and volunteered to carpool while I'm living nearby. I think that will be okay."

"I'll call them on my way to work."

"What can I make for you for breakfast?" She asks again, grimacing as she takes a sip of her black coffee.

The look on her face makes me chuckle. "Do you have a sweet tooth?"

She adds two generous spoonfuls of sugar to her cup. Then she adds skim milk, takes another sip, and is placated for the moment. "I do, but it looks like you try to eat healthily, so I will refrain from bringing a bunch of junk into the house."

I take a couple of steps to the left and open up a cabinet that is eye level with my six foot seven height. "All the junk is in here. Nyla and I have a cheat day once a week, usually on Tuesdays, which is my only actual day off. Of course, she's welcome to have whatever, whenever, but I think she enjoys making it a thing for us to look forward to together."

Downing the last of my smoothie, I put the container in the dishwasher. Then I grab a couple of whole-grain waffles out of the freezer and pop them in the toaster. "As far as breakfast is concerned, when I'm in town, I'll make it. I get so little time with Nyla, and it's the only meal I know I'm going to be here for. You can take care of lunch and dinner, but right now our go-to breakfast is waffle sandwiches. Would you like one?" I flash her a teasing grin.

She nods enthusiastically. "Absolutely."

Without having to wake her up, Nyla comes shuffling

down the stairs with her brush in hand. My little girl is also not a morning person, and her eyes bounce from me to Sunshine and back again.

"Good morning, Princess."

Nyla grumbles and hands Sunshine her brush. "Can you fix my braid?"

"Of course, I can."

"Hey, where is my good morning?" I pout and toss her a hurt look.

Nyla flings herself against my legs and hugs them, her face smashed between my knees. "I'm tired."

"Then why are you up?" I rub small circles over her shoulder blades.

"Because I heard you guys talking, and I wanted to be part of the conversation."

"Oh—" I roll my eyes "—you are always afraid you're going to miss something."

Sunshine stands behind Nyla and removes the braid, brushing her hair as I grab a couple of slices of Canadian bacon and three eggs out of the refrigerator. This entire morning feels so natural, as if we've been doing it for months.

It's been one night. Less than twenty-four hours. We should not be this comfortable with each other, and yet this feels easy.

Less than ten minutes later, we're sitting down like a family and eating our breakfast sandwiches. Sunshine clears our plates and then shoos me out of the kitchen when I attempt to do the dishes. "I got this. Go get ready for your day."

When I come down the stairs with my gym bag, Nyla is handing me a lunch bag with a huge smile on her face. "We packed your snacks."

"You did?" I chuckle, taking the insulated bag from her and placing a kiss on her cheek. "Thank you, Princess. Now go brush your teeth and get dressed. Mind Miss Sunshine and have a good day at school."

"Of course, Daddy." Nyla runs up the stairs at the same time Sunshine walks out of her bedroom as I'm approaching the garage door.

I walk toward her and then course correct, realizing I almost leaned in on auto-pilot to kiss her goodbye. "Uh, if you need anything today, text me."

"Same. Have a good practice." Sunshine holds the garage door open for me as if she's waiting for that kiss. "See you tonight."

Wow. There is something about knowing she'll be here when I get home that makes me dread the long day ahead. Thirteen hours before I'll see her warm smile and dazzling energy again—that's too long.

"See you tonight."

Sunshine texts me a couple of hours later.

I talked to the teacher, Mrs. Abreton. She's cool and I know will keep our secret. She said as a teacher's aide, there shouldn't be a problem with me living with you and taking care of Nyla, as long as I don't show preferential treatment in class. Considering this is kindergarten, I'm not worried. So I would like to talk about a more permanent arrangement, maybe after a few days or weeks of this trial run. Ya know, so I'm not paying rent some place I'm not living and you have some stability in your life. I'm going to leave Nyla at school with the teacher and run back to my apartment for lunch so I can grab a couple of weeks' worth of clothing and stuff.

Grab it all. Come live with us full-time. Tell your roommate you're moving out. Unless you have big secrets you are hiding from me, I think we can make this arrangement work, don't you?

<3 I do, but we should still discuss it with Nyla.

Okay, we'll give it the weekend. Speaking of which, how would you feel about bringing Nyla to the game on Sunday? I don't have a private box or anything, but there are a few wives who bring their kids to play and watch the game at the stadium. Brenda didn't want to be burdened with Nyla's safety at a large public event, but I would like her to come to as many home games as she wants.

Are you kidding me? I would LOVE that.

Do you know football?

I know hot men in tight pants run up and down a field tackling each other. What else do I need to know?

Fair point.

A wide, goofy grin spreads across my face as I ignore my chicken stir-fry.

"Who are you texting with that big smile on your face?" Declan Scott sits down next to me with his tray of food. The star quarterback never sits with me, so I put my phone face down and shake my head.

Devlin Frank, the number one receiver in the league, sits across from him. "We can see your smile from across the room. What's up?"

I shrug like it's no big deal and I don't have butterflies dancing around in my belly. "New nanny. That's why I took off early yesterday. My nanny quit without telling me, leaving my little girl stranded at school. Luckily, the teacher's aide stayed with her. We went to dinner last night and next thing I know, she's moving in."

They exchange a look as Aggie sits in front of me next to Devlin. This is weird. These guys never sit with me. I'm on the defense. They are offense. Not that there's a rule or something about us commingling. It just doesn't happen a lot.

"Is she hot?" Declan waggles his brow.

I pick up my fork and spear a couple of chunks of chicken. "She's attractive."

"Awww, yeah." He chuckles and takes a big bite of his sandwich.

Shaking my head, I shove my mouth full of chicken and vegetables, giving me a reason to think through my response. "It's not like that, man. Nyla loves her, and I need someone reliable or else I'm going to have to quit playing ball."

Deacon Scott, the guy who recruited me despite our run-in on the field three and a half years ago, sits next to his younger brother, Declan. "What are you talking about?"

Declan speaks for me. "Rylie—a single dad as well as an outstanding defensive back—is having a hard time keeping reliable childcare for his daughter, and I doubt thirteen-hour days six days a week are helping the matter."

So, that was using my situation to dig at management on the team's behalf. I wonder what it is like to be a player and an owner at the same time. Are the Scott's allegiances divided? Do they get into arguments over family dinners on the regular?

Deacon sighs. "I know, man. I'm working on it."

"It's been five weeks, bro. This is ridiculous. Some of us don't have a woman waiting for us at home and need to get laid." Declan grumbles before taking another big bite of his sandwich.

As if thinking about his new fiancée sparks a memory, Deacon's cheeks redden and a big smile spreads across his face. "You're just mad because you can't sweet talk that reporter while the no-contact edict is in place."

"Oh, I will be soon enough. You can put money on that."

This is fascinating. I've never hung out with the Scotts as they talk to each other as brothers. Obviously, Deacon and I have had quite a few conversations over the years. I spent many afternoons hanging out with him at the hospital and even offered to help him through rehab after the incident. The memory of that day on the field still haunts me, and even though it was a clean hit, it affected my playing for the next few years. Deacon's the reason I'm here now, because he watched me temper myself on the field, and knew I was at risk of being let go if I didn't play to my full potential. The Rangers' defensive coordinators are harder on me for that exact reason, but I knew that walking onto the team.

"Back to you, Rylie." Deacon rolls his eyes and pushes past his brother to look me in the eye. "If you need childcare, come to us and we'll help you figure something out. You are the only single father with full parental custody on our team, and probably one of only a handful in the league. We take care of our own."

"Thanks." I blush a little. Being a player with the Denver Mustangs was cool, but they aren't like the Rangers. I doubt many teams are considering none of them are family owned. This is the last privately owned team in the league. "I think I have it handled for now, but if that changes, I'll let you know."

Aggie, who hasn't said a word throughout all of this, nods his head in my direction. In a lot of ways, we have similar stories. We're two of the biggest players on the team, and we both have nightmares for ex-wives, although the rumor mill says Aggie's ex is a lot more vindictive than mine. Heather is intent on ruining her own life, while Ellen is determined to ruin Aggie's. Poor bastard. At least he doesn't have a child with her. I can only imagine the games she would play with a kid as leverage.

"Well, if you need help, you have my number." Deacon stands up and smacks her brother on the back of the head. Declan swings back, just missing contact with Deacon's nuts.

Ahhhh... to have a brother.

Chapter 4
Sunshine

I packed most of my stuff during my lunch hour and gave my roommate notice to look for a new occupant. Considering she rented me a furnished bedroom on a month-to-month lease, I'm not worried about moving big items. One more trip next week will wrap up anything I left behind today.

The entire situation must have been bothering me more than I realized because after I sent that text, I felt like I could breathe for the first time in weeks. Maybe moving in with Rylie and Nyla seems like a hasty decision to the outside observer, but I've been working with Nyla for six weeks now and I adore her. Rylie, if he was intolerable, would be a mild inconvenience, considering he's never home. Lucky for me, he's not only tolerable but dreamy in a completely off-limits kind of way. I don't want to make life uncomfortable for him, so I'll keep my flirting down to a minimum.

Nyla and I are sitting in her room while she brushes my hair when we hear the garage door open.

"He's late." Nyla tsks.

"I'm sure he worked very hard today."

"Let's hide from him." She giggles, jumping off the chair and running to her closet, leaving me with nowhere to go. I duck out of her room and into his, closing the door partially behind me. I haven't been in his room yet. There are artsy black and whites of a partially nude female adorning the walls, capturing my attention. They are racier than the black and white photos in the living and dining room, but no less artful.

"Where's my princess?" Rylie says, his voice right outside the door.

"Rawr!" Nyla jumps out, giggling as I presume he picks her up and swings her around.

"Where is Miss Sunshine?"

"She's hiding too, Daddy. Find her."

Shit! Now I wish I hadn't hidden in his room. I feel like I'm violating his trust—big time.

I slap my hands over my eyes as he pushes the door open slowly, pinning me in place behind it.

"Where could she be?" He taunts.

Nyla giggles as I peek through my splayed fingers to find Rylie looking at me with his eyebrow cocked. "Found you."

"Sorry. She sprung hiding from you on me and I know shouldn't be in your room, but I didn't know where to go."

"You kind of suck at this game." He chuckles.

"You're not mad that I'm in your room?"

"I have nothing to hide, Sunshine." His eyes lock with mine and I feel like there's more he wants to say. He smiles and then turns away, carrying Nyla back to her room and bidding me to follow them. Tucking her in bed, he sits on the edge as I take his place from last night in the big chair. "How was your day, Princess?"

"Good. We finger painted today."

"Oh yeah? Did you bring home some new artwork for me?"

Nyla curls her lips. "No. None of it was good enough."

I roll my eyes. "She's very hard on herself, but I have them downstairs for your collection."

"That's my girl." His cheeks turn red as he shakes his head and turns wide eyes my way. "Sorry, I didn't mean it like that."

I bite my lip, a rare blush also hitting my cheeks. "It's okay. I know what you meant."

Getting up from the chair, I throw Nyla a wink. "I'm going to get ready for bed, but I'll see you in the morning, sweetie."

"Night, Miss Sunshine."

In the kitchen, I pull out a container of tonight's spaghetti ragu and wait for Rylie. I only have to wait a few minutes before he comes down, his eyes locking with mine. "How was your first day?"

"It was good. Nyla's super easy to take care of, and she's a lot of fun, too."

"Good. I got you two tickets for Sunday's game and a special parking pass."

"Okay." I motion to the container. "We had spaghetti tonight. Do you want me to warm you up a plate?"

He shakes his head. "Not tonight, but I'll take it with me for lunch tomorrow."

"Can I get you a chocolate protein shake instead? I saw you have them in the bottom drawer." I waggle my brows like I'm tempting him with something forbidden. It's not what I want to tempt him with, but if we're going to turn this into a long-term employment sitch, I need to keep it in my pants.

Leaning his hips against the counter, he crosses his arms over his massive chest. Good lord, the size of this man is enough to make a girl's knees go weak. "You've learned my weakness."

"Hopefully, it's not the only one." I hand him a chocolate shake.

He cracks open the bottle and drinks it down in three long gulps, his eyes not leaving me once. Grabbing a paper towel, he wipes his mouth and then washes his hands and rinses out the bottle before tossing it in the recycling bin. One thing about this man, he's meticulous. The schedule and routine, the cleanliness of his house, the organization of his cupboards and refrigerator—not what I would expect from a single father with a five-year-old daughter.

Is it a case of OCD or something else? I'm not sure, but I hope I can keep up with his expectations.

"The black and white pictures throughout the house—did you take them?"

He nods, a shyness crossing over his face. "Yeah. I've always been interested in photography."

"They are very good. I especially like the ones in your room."

"Hopefully they are abstract enough that five-year-olds don't understand what they are looking at."

"Oh yeah, I didn't see it at first, but then I did. Who was she?"

"A model from my art class in college. She wasn't nude, but damn well near."

"Ever take pictures of someone you know?" I can't believe I'm asking him this. His answer could take us into flirty territory quickly as we stand a few feet away from each other. The denied chemistry between us is very real. I feel it, and I'm sure he does too.

"There were some of my ex-wife, but I gave her those and I'm sure she either sold them or trashed them."

I bite my lip and cast my eyes to my bare feet. "If you took pictures of me, I wouldn't trash them. I would treasure them."

When he says nothing, I bring my eyes up. He's resumed his pose with his arms crossed over his chest, and although his eyes are on me, he is slowly shaking his head. "That's a conversation for another time."

"We seem to rack those up."

"I need you." He closes his eyes and swallows the lump in his throat. "Nyla and I need you, and I don't want to complicate our business arrangement with sex."

"I understand." I nod, disappointment slithering through my veins. He's right, but that doesn't dampen my attraction to him in the slightest. "Can we revisit the conversation from yesterday about Nyla's mother?"

"It's certainly a safer topic."

"You mentioned she had a drug possession charge last year. Is that what broke you up?"

"Amongst other things. Heather was a partier when I met her, but what I didn't know was that she was also an addict. I think she tried in the beginning, but certain lifestyles get their hooks in you and never let go. Before we met, she used her jobs at the bar and at the lingerie shop to interview clients who she would later meet up with for a night of partying. Stripping, escorting, drinking, drugs—you name it. I didn't know any of this in the beginning, but it all came out in the end when she no longer cared to hide it."

"It seems like, maybe, she knew she was an unfit mother, and that's why she removed herself from Nyla's life?"

He shrugs. "It doesn't matter if she realizes it or not. I can't believe a word that comes out of her mouth, anyway. I can forgive almost anything except for a blatant lie. Especially after I gave her so many chances to come clean and tell me the truth so we'd get help together."

"Will she ever see her daughter again?"

"Yeah, but only via supervised visits with her parents. I can barely stand to be in the same room with her right now, but her parents are wonderful people and ask to see Nyla once or twice a month. So, occasionally you'll get a night off when I am out of town and the grandparents want her to spend the night. I think deep down Heather loves her, but she knows she's no good for her."

I step forward and slide my hands up his thick biceps, rubbing his arms reassuringly. "I'm so sorry you had to go through that."

Rylie's muscles tense under my fingertips and his sharp intake of breath brings my eyes up to his face. "I should go to bed."

Nodding, I take a step back. "Yeah, me too. What's the rule on Saturdays? Do we get up with you, or can we sleep in and catch morning cartoons?"

He smiles. "Sleep in. I'll try to be quiet as I leave the house."

"Okay. Sleep well, Rylie."

"You too, Sunshine."

I wake up to cartoon characters screaming on the TV and glance at my phone to check the time.

Oh crap, it's eight!

Jumping out of bed, I poke my head out of my room to find Nyla sitting on the couch in her PJs under a throw blanket with a lapboard.

"Good morning, sweetie. I'm sorry I overslept."

Nyla looks up from her coloring book. "You were tired."

"I guess I was. Are you hungry?"

She nods enthusiastically.

"Is it pancake day?"

"Definitely."

After breakfast, I jump in the shower and check my phone for text messages. None from Rylie, which I guess means they are having a full day. He mentioned he usually only has his phone on him at lunch, but his watch will alert him if I send an emergency message.

"Have you ever had a pedicure, Nyla?" I come out of my bedroom brushing my damp, freshly showered hair.

"Yes, but I need a new one."

"Want to go to the mall and get a pedicure and maybe a pretzel?"

"Okay!" Nyla jumps off the couch and runs to the stairs.

I giggle at her enthusiasm. "Do you need help picking out an outfit?"

"No, but will you put my hair up in pigtails?"

"I sure will. I'll be up in a minute."

Two hours later, we're sitting in pedicure chairs and I'm scrolling through my bank account on my phone. I need to send Tony another loan payment, but I know as soon as I do, he'll call me. I've been ducking his calls for weeks now, making payments on the sly without confronting my desire to not work off any of my remaining debt by dancing in his clubs. While in college, I danced a few times a month to pay my bills not covered by scholarships and grants, and that was fine while I was a student. But now that I'm a teacher, I can't risk anyone recognizing me—although the risk is low considering the clubs are in Denver and I always wear a wig and a ridiculous amount of makeup when I perform.

Still.

Tony's not a bad man. He owns a handful of gentlemen's clubs up in Denver and always lets me do a burlesque-style routine versus a straight strip tease. I undress to my comfort level, which is pasties and g-strings. My onstage persona for the last few years has been Rainbow, and I've danced at least once at all of his clubs, usually filling in at the last minute for a dancer who called in sick. In the end, my style of performance best fit in with the crowd at Diamonds and Pearls, which is a more sophisticated clientele.

Tony runs clean establishments, and he's a good guy. One girl in my hall my sophomore year, Alexxi, introduced me to him when my scholarships and grant monies came up short. I had enough to pay for tuition, books, and my room, but if I wanted to eat or grab essentials like shampoo and toothpaste, I had to find a job. Most college students take five years to graduate nowadays, but I knew I didn't have the backing to support that and had to finish in four—therefore taking time away from my studies by getting a part-time minimum wage job left little to be desired. Or, as Alexxi pointed out, I could dance two or three nights a month and make a thousand dollars easily.

I don't make nearly as much as the full-time dancers because I don't do private rooms or lap dances. I'm strictly an onstage three times over three hours kind of girl—usually on a weeknight, so I average around five hundred dollars.

Still... It was easy money without a lot of time, and a bonus because it was all under the table. Nothing on my credit report or background check.

Alexxi's way seemed like the smartest option, and it was for a long time. I don't regret a minute of it. The overall experience was positive, especially under Tony's care, but it's not the life for me.

Unfortunately, halfway through my senior year, my scholarship didn't come through and I was too late to apply for financial aid. I had to come up with my last semester tuition fast or else I would be unenrolled from my classes and miss my graduation window. Tony, who never loans money, offered me a fair deal. Ten thousand dollar loan paid back before the end of the year. Of course, I'm paying back almost double, but without him, I never would've graduated on time. Looking at my account, knowing I'm a couple of months behind, which means penalties, which also means god knows how much I still owe. Eight grand, maybe?

At least I can give him a full payment this month.

I bring up my PayPal and send him fifteen hundred dollars. The only reason I have money this month is because Rylie put it in my account yesterday.

As predicted, my phone rings two minutes later.

I glance at Nyla and roll my eyes dramatically. "Hang tight. I need to take this phone call."

She giggles and nods like she's in on the conspiracy.

"Hey you," I answer with the chipperness expected from a person with the name Sunshine.

"I just got your payment. I have to say, I thought you were avoiding me."

"No, Tony, of course not. I'm sorry, but the move to Spring City has been crazier than I thought it would be, and setting up in a new residence broke me more than I expected."

"You know the best way to deal with being broke is to come in and work." He says flatly.

"I know, but I got a job nannying, which means my nights are not my own anymore."

He sighs. "Look Sunshine, I know dancing in a club is not your future, and because you're working with kids and stuff you've got to keep it on the down low, but we had a deal and you know this is why I don't loan money."

"I know. With this new job, I can get you at least five grand by Christmas."

"Yeah, but you owe me seventy-five hundred, considering you haven't paid me for the last three months. Our deal was simple. Fifteen hundred dollars a month for twelve months and we're square. Anything less than fifteen hundred, and I doubled and added it to the next month. You missed three months, so that's an additional forty-five hundred you owe me. Every night you show up for work is a guaranteed five hundred off of your bill regardless of what you made in tips that night. Now, you're pushing into next year, and we'll have to renegotiate our terms."

My enthusiasm deflates. He's not wrong, and he's been more than patient and fair with me. "I'm taking care of a fantastic kid and I don't want to screw it up. Let me talk to my new employer about getting a couple of days off so I can come up there. Okay?"

Tony's voice is firm yet gentle. "I'll tell you what, Sunshine. We've got this big party coming up in three weeks—on a Monday night of all nights—and I have to move some girls around so I can cover the craziness going down at the Rawhide. That's going to leave me short at the other clubs. If you come up here Monday night and help me out, I'll triple whatever you make that night and apply it to your debt."

"Monday the twenty-fifth?"

"Yeah. There's some national ranchers association bullshit convention going on in Loveland, but they're coming down here to party. Lots of money. Lots of liquor. And lots of girls requested."

I imagine Tony rolling his eyes. As I said, he's not a bad guy, but he does not play with his money.

"I'll ask for the night off and send you a text later."

"Okay. Talk to you then."

"Thanks, Tony."

I hang up the phone and look back at the pedicure chairs where a chatty Nyla rambles on to the nail tech without care. I don't want to mess up this opportunity, nor do I want to betray Rylie, but I have a debt to pay.

One more time. One more night. I can do this, and then I'll have no more secrets from Rylie, Nyla, or myself.

Chapter 5
Rylie

It's been three weeks since Sunshine came into our lives, and I'm equally relieved and frustrated. Night after night I come home to a clean house, a happy Nyla, and a friendly, somewhat flirty Sunshine. If we were free to be together, I know exactly what we'd be doing once Nyla fell asleep every night.

Instead, I'm fisting my cock once before bed and again before breakfast. She's the perfect woman for a single father like me because she understands Nyla has to come first, no matter what. And I believe she would let Nyla be first in both of our lives if we were together, taking care of her and me while I take care of my daughter and her.

I know she cares for my little girl like she's her own, and I couldn't ask for more from a nanny, girlfriend, or wife.

But would crossing this invisible line between us ruin

everything? Maybe the sexual tension wrapped around us, once sated, would reveal a bunch of things we don't like about each other.

I can't risk it.

"Welcome home." Sunshine is in the kitchen dishing up bowls of ice cream. She holds up the scoop when I walk in. "Want a lick?"

I'm used to her double entendres and subtle suggestive comments. Honestly, I don't think she's cognizant of half the things that come out of her mouth until they are already in the air between us. Or, if she is, she plays them off as innocent very well.

"I'll take a scoop." I flash her a knowing smile before dropping my bag at the foot of the stairs. It's Friday night and Nyla is sitting on the couch with a movie paused instead of in bed, waiting for her bedtime story.

"Hey, Daddy."

"Hey, Princess." I plop down next to her and pull her into my lap. "How was school today?"

"Good. How was practice?"

"Also good."

"Did you make good tackles today?"

I chuckle. "I got a couple of good ones in. What are we watching?"

"Minions."

"Again?" I glance at Sunshine as she sets down two bowls of ice cream. "Thanks."

"You are welcome. Do you also want a protein shake?"

"No, I'm good." She's always trying to feed me. I pat

the couch cushion next to me. "Sit down and start the movie."

As soon as she's seated, I grab the remote and dim the overhead lights, pulling the blanket up over Nyla, who took over my lap. She takes a couple of bites of her ice cream, but as usual, I end up eating most of hers as well as my own. I don't know why I even ask for a separate bowl.

Sunshine moves to gather our dishes and I wrap my hand over the top of her thigh, holding her next to me on the couch. "Leave it and relax with us."

It takes maybe another fifteen minutes before Nyla has shifted her position and is splayed across my chest, fast asleep. Sunshine has her feet tucked up underneath her, so her body leans against mine while I drape my arm behind her over the top of the couch. I could fall asleep like this. It's comfortable with Sunshine's head resting against my shoulder, her breath caressing my pec.

I think Sunshine feels it too because she lifts her head and looks at me, her eyes searching my face before she looks down at Nyla. "Out cold, as per usual."

"Yeah, she's a good sleeper."

"I wanted to talk to you about her birthday in two weeks. Five-year-old celebrations are a big deal, and I thought since I know her classmates, I could schedule something at Gymboree and invite some of her friends."

A birthday party?

An actual birthday party with friends and presents and cake?

I could kiss Sunshine right now.

"What day were you thinking?"

"Well, we could do it after school a week from Tuesday. That way you could attend."

I let my arm fall around her shoulder and pull her close, kissing her forehead. "You are a godsend, you know that?"

"Is that a yes?"

"It's perfect and something I could not do without you."

"You know, Nyla expressed an interest in gymnastics the other day. Have you thought about enrolling her in any activities?"

"Well, sure, I've thought about it, but I can't take her to those things. And I didn't want to ask you until we were in a much more stable situation."

"I feel pretty stable." She smiles up at me.

"Things have been going well."

"How about I research a couple of things and bring them to you before we talk to her about them? I can gather up all the information about classes and schedules and costs, and you tell me what you think."

My heart feels like it's about to burst out of my chest. Nyla has never complained once, but I knew at some point extracurricular activities were going to come up. "I'd like to get her involved in swimming as well."

"Anything you want, I'm here to take care of."

Taking a deep breath, I let it out slowly and move my arm from her shoulder. I want her so fucking badly, and I'm too tired to fight my urges. "I'm going to put Nyla to bed."

Sunshine pushes back from me and nods. "Okay."

After tucking my daughter in, I come down the stairs to find Sunshine in the kitchen cleaning up our ice cream. I lean my hip against the counter and cross my arms over my chest again, a common stance I take to keep myself from reaching out for her. "Is this working out for you—living here and taking care of Nyla?"

"I'm happy, are you?"

"Everything is perfect. You make my life easy."

She smiles. "Well good. That's my job."

"You have plans on Monday night, right?"

She bites her lip. "Yeah, I need to take care of something with one of my college girlfriends until about midnight, but then I'll be home after that. Do you need me for something?"

"No. Nyla's grandparents have been asking for her, so I might run her up there for dinner or something."

"Do you think you'll be around for trick-or-treating?"

"Shit, it is almost the end of October, isn't it? Do I need to get Nyla a costume?"

Sunshine shakes her head. "Oh no, we already have it handled, and it's a big surprise."

"A surprise?"

Sunshine gets a devious smile on her face. "Oh yes. We got you a costume too if you're available."

"What is it?"

She shakes her head and presses her lips together. "I'm not telling. You'll have to torture it out of me."

I move without thinking, wrapping my big hands around her waist to tickle it out of her.

She yelps. I pull her into my body; her ass nestled perfectly against my hardening cock, and hiss in her ear. "Shhh. You'll wake Nyla."

Neither of us moves as Sunshine sucks in her breath and turns her face to mine. Her lips are so close, and yet still, we don't move a fraction of an inch.

"It's becoming harder to ignore the tension between us."

"Yeah," is all she says.

"Crossing the professional line is a bad idea."

"Maybe." she says, "but I want to, anyway."

I close my eyes and let her go. "I should go to bed."

She sighs. "If that's what you have to do."

"What else am I supposed to do, Sunshine?" Fuck, I'm so damn frustrated I can't think straight. I've never been so tempted by someone I know I should deny myself. If she didn't want me too, this would be easy, but she doesn't seem interested in denying herself at all.

She takes several steps toward her bedroom and away from me. "I don't know. I understand your concerns, but you act like you're the only one with something to lose here. If you were to decide tomorrow that this isn't working, where am I going to go? I have no family or friends here, and I gave up my apartment for you and Nyla. I know you wouldn't kick me out on my ass, but it's not a decision that can be made lightly for either of us. And then there's Nyla. I adore her, and it would break me to see her at school and know I'm not taking care of her as I should be." She brings her head up and pins me in place with light brown eyes shimmering with unshed tears. "And we won't even talk about my feelings for you."

I'm across the room in four long strides, cupping her face in my callused hands. She grips my upper arms, her fingers digging into my biceps, her lips parted in surprise.

"You're not the only one struggling with your feelings."

"Who said I was struggling?" She licks her lips, and her eyes burn into me with a fiery passion. "I don't believe you are anything other than who I think you are—a doting father and amazing man, who is way sexier than he knows. I want to be part of your life, to take care of you and Nyla like I do now, but I also want you in my bed. You want me to deny my attraction to you, but I can't. I've wanted you from day one and I don't foresee my feelings changing."

I swipe my thumb across her lower lip and lean my forehead against hers. "If we let ourselves go there, it's not just about us. Nyla might love you, but that doesn't mean she'll love us together. She's never seen me with someone, and I have no idea how she would react."

Sunshine grabs two handfuls of my shirt and presses her lush curves against my body. She hits me with a small smile and a sarcastic arch of her brow. "Are you committed to being a celibate bachelor until she's gone away to college?"

Shaking my head, I try not to chuckle. "I don't know. I haven't thought that far ahead."

"We don't have to tell Nyla until we know where we,

as two consenting adults, are taking this thing. Who knows? You might hate sliding between my thighs."

Sucking in my breath, I fist a handful of her hair, my lips barely brushing against hers. "I seriously doubt that."

Tentatively, she sticks out her tongue and licks my lips, her voice husky and eyes aflame with a teasing glint. "Maybe riding your cock won't live up to my fantasies."

I run my hand down her spine and palm her ass, pressing my erection into her soft core. "I'll make sure you like it even more."

She moans softly, swiveling her hips against me. "Do you have any idea how many times I have fucked my vibrator and groaned your name into my pillow at night?"

"Goddammit Sunshine." My control snaps. Cupping her ass, I lift her, giving her no choice but to wrap her legs around my waist.

"Daddy?" Nyla calls from her bedroom upstairs.

"Shit." Sunshine whispers.

"Yeah, Princess?" I call over my shoulder, but my gaze, my focus, is on the lush woman in my arms.

"Can you come here, please?"

Sunshine nods, dropping her legs from my hips. "Nyla comes first. I'll be in my room—if you want me."

"What's up, Princess?" I walk into Nyla's room, her night light casting shadows across the walls.

"What were you doing?" She has her arms wrapped around her stuffed llama—a toy Sunshine got for her a few weeks ago.

"Talking. Why?"

"Do you like Miss Sunshine?"

I sink into the big chair in the corner. "Yes, don't you?"

"Yes, but it's more than that, Daddy. I don't just like her. I love her."

"I'm pretty sure she loves you, too."

"Do you know what I'm gonna wish for when I blow out my birthday candles?"

I sigh, wondering where this is going. "What's that, Princess?"

"I'm gonna wish for a mommy who loves me the same way I love her."

Her pained, innocent words make my heart and spirit break. Any residual blood feeding my cock from being seconds away from touching and tasting Sunshine for the first time comes back to my brain. I get up and cross the tiny room, sitting next to my daughter on her little twin bed. With my back propped up against the headboard, I put my arm around her and pull her to my side so she can lay her head on my thigh.

I feel the silent tears seep through my sweatpants. Anger and sadness swirl into an emotional stew that sits heavy in my gut.

Fucking Heather.

Stroking Nyla's hair, I keep my voice soft. "Remember when we talked about priorities, and how there are many ways to show others' love and affection and one of those ways is by making them a priority?"

"Yeah." She sniffles.

"Well, you are going to have so many people who love you throughout your life. When you are young, it will often be a maternal love, whether they're your grandma, mommy, aunt, or other women who want to protect, love, and mentor you. Your mommy Heather loves you, but she doesn't know how to prioritize others over herself."

"She's selfish." Hurt and resentment lace Nyla's tone.

I sigh. "Yeah, I guess she is. But you know, Nyla, she's the one missing out, and I know it makes you sad, but you can't force somebody to love you the way you want to be loved."

"But everyone else at school has a mommy. A couple of the kids have two. I'm the only one that only has a daddy."

I shake my head. "I don't know what to say to that, Nyla, except I'm sorry."

"I didn't say that to make you feel bad, Daddy. It's just something I think about sometimes."

"Is that why you're awake after bedtime?"

"Yeah. I had a bad dream, and I woke up sad."

"Do you want to tell me about your bad dream?"

She sighs. "I was lost at the store yelling for Mommy, but she never came."

Closing my eyes, I wrap my arms around her tighter. "I love you so much, Nyla. Miss Sunshine loves you. Nammy and Pappa love you. Your uncle Sammy loves you. All your friends at school love you. As a matter of fact, I don't think there's been one person who has met you that doesn't love you."

"I know, Daddy. I love them too."

"I need you to sleep now, Princess. Can you do it for me?"

"Yeah. I'm feeling pretty tired now."

"I'll see you in the morning."

Outside of Nyla's door, I debate going back downstairs. I can't screw up things with Sunshine, but her words weigh on my mind. I'm not the only one with something to lose here, and to be honest, I care about her, too.

I'm walking down the stairs before I even know my feet are moving in her direction. Sunshine's door is slightly ajar, and she's laying on her side facing the door with her phone in her hand. "Is everything okay?"

Her brow furrows as she takes in my expression. "No, it's not okay. What's wrong?"

"Has Nyla told you she loves you?"

Sunshine sits up and puts her phone down, nodding slowly, "Yeah, last week."

"What did you say?"

"I told her I love her too."

"Do you?"

"Yes. Of course. I never would have said it, except she surprised me and I reacted, but I absolutely meant it. I love your little girl. She's an absolute joy to be around. Why? What's wrong?"

Shaking my head, I let my breath out slowly as I think through my words. "I want you, but I'm afraid I'll hurt Nyla, you, or myself, if I have you." I run my hand through my hair and lean against her door frame. "My little girl is sad right now, and I can't risk hurting her more."

Sunshine stands up and takes my hand. "Come here."

I don't have the energy to fight her. "We shouldn't do this tonight."

She narrows her eyes and shakes her head, leading me to the bed. "Shut up, relax, and let someone care for you for once."

Then she does something unexpected. She curls up next to me on the bed and wraps her arms around me.

"What are we doing?" I tense as her freshly washed hair and citrus-scented shampoo fill my nostrils and she lays her head and hand on my chest.

"Cuddling." She says nonchalantly.

"Cuddling?" I scoff but wrap my arms tighter around her.

She feels so good.

This feels so good.

"Yeah, the laying down version of hugging. You need a hug, and I want to give you one."

Her warmth infuses my muscles as all the stress melts from my body. I wiggle until I am lying comfortably on her bed, and she pulls the blanket up over us. We're both fully dressed—me in a T-shirt and sweatpants, her in a tank top and sleep shorts—and yet, this feels more intimate than I've been in years.

Sunshine doesn't speak, she doesn't let her hands roam, or move her lips near exposed skin. She simply holds me and lets me hold her until we both fall fast asleep.

Chapter 6

Sunshine

Rylie left my bed just before five, but not before rolling me to my back and kissing me softly, making me a solemn promise that we will find time to explore each other when he gets back from Seattle.

I can't wait.

Nyla and I spend Saturday checking out Gymboree. We schedule her party for the following Tuesday, which gives us one week to invite everyone. Then we go to the party supply store and pick out her birthday theme—a combination of minions and football. We even found plates and cups that had both.

"Miss Sunshine?" Nyla says between sips of her orange-sprite-root beer combination she made herself at McDs.

"Yes, sweetie?"

"Could I call you mommy someday?"

I pause with my chicken sandwich raised to my

mouth. "Uh, I'm not sure that's a good idea while we are in kindergarten together. It might make the other kids jealous."

She nods thoughtfully. "That's true. What about after when you're no longer my teacher?"

"Well, why don't we talk about it, then?" I push one of her blonde curls out of her face as she lifts a ketchup-smothered french fry to her mouth. "What brought this question on?"

"I don't want to invite my real mommy to my birthday, but there will be other mommies there, and I want to say somebody is my mommy."

"Oh, sweetie." I pull her close and kiss her temple. "You'll have your daddy, nammy, pappa, and me there, and we all love you. I think everyone will know how much we love you without introducing any of us as your mommy. And if someone asks, you just point to any of us and say they are who love and take care of me."

Six hours later, Nyla and I are winding down from our day when my phone rings.

I glance at the screen and then at Nyla. "It's your daddy."

She answers the phone by putting it on speaker. "Hi, Daddy."

"Hey, Princess. Did you have fun today?"

"Yeah. We went shopping for my birthday party decorations."

"What did you decide on?"

"Minions."

"Again?" He teases.

She giggles. "Yes, again."

"Are you ready for bed?"

"Yeah. Are you ready to play football?"

"Tomorrow night, Princess. I'll call you before we play, but I won't get home until well after midnight. Nammy wants to see you, so I was thinking we can have dinner with them after school on Monday."

"Okay. Good night, Daddy."

"Good night, Princess. Good night, Miss Sunshine." I can hear his smile through the phone.

"Good night, Rylie. Sleep well."

"Probably not as well as last night, but I'll do my best." His voice is deep and husky and has my pussy clenching in anticipation.

I turn away from Nyla to hide my smile. Although I've been lusting after him for weeks, there is something about spending the night in the arms of the man you care about with no sexual contact. The night did not dampen my desires, but I feel closer to him than before, as if we share an intimacy stronger than sex. He is mine to care for, cherish, protect, and if he lets me, love.

Because I'm positive I'm falling in love with Rylie Reynolds, just as sure as I am that I love his daughter Nyla like she is my own.

Rylie ended up not getting home until Monday morning while Nyla and I were at school because of the weather in Seattle. Tonight I have to pay my debt—my last night dancing—to Tony, and then I'm free to pursue whatever future there is for me here in Spring City. Does it include a life with Rylie and an adorable little five-year-old? I hope so. But, regardless, this is the only thing I have hanging over my head, and I'm ready to finish it.

Part of me wants to tell Rylie about my plans tonight because I feel awful withholding from him, but once this is over, I never have to think about it again. No one knows about my dancing except for my college girlfriend Alexxi, who I rarely keep in contact with anymore. Obviously, Tony knows, but he would never tell.

"Have fun with your friends tonight." Rylie watches me from the kitchen as I sling my duffel bag over my shoulder. "If you drink too much, call me and I'll give you a ride."

"It's not like that. I won't be drinking tonight."

He nods. "Well, if you need me, you know how to get in touch with me."

I bite my lip and take a step towards him—the truth about to spill from my lips when Nyla comes running up from the basement.

"I'm ready to go!" she exclaims, super excited about seeing her nammy.

"You guys have fun tonight."

"We will see you in the morning." His eyes tell me I'll

be seeing him tonight if he hears me when I come home. I can't wait.

"Yeah."

It's a forty-five-minute drive on a good day, but I hit rush hour, which means it takes me almost an hour and a half to get downtown where the club is located. I pull into the back where all of the dancers park; the area covered by cameras and monitored by security. Knocking on the back door, a big guy I don't recognize opens it. I haven't been here in months, and the security around here changes almost as often as the dancers.

Walking down the hallway, I stop at the manager's door and poke my head in. "Hey, Tony."

"Sunshine. You made it." He flashes me a warm smile. As I said, he's not a bad guy.

"As promised. Do you know when I'm dancing tonight?"

"Yeah, we'll put you on once an hour until eleven. I'm leaving here in a few minutes to go up to Rawhide and make sure they set everything for tonight, but I'll be back before you leave."

"Okay."

"You got your props with you?" He eyes my duffel bag.

"A few. I'll have to make do tonight considering my roommate threw out most of my stuff when I canceled my month-to-month lease and her boyfriend mysteriously broke up with her two days later."

"What?" He furrows his brow.

I shake my head and wave away his concern. "Nothing. Just some guy that I think was maybe stalking me by dating her so he could gain access to our apartment. It's this long boring story... you know how it goes."

He narrows his eyes. Tony used to be a cop, runs a handful of clubs now, and has a lifetime of knowing creeps. His wife was a dancer and is now a manager, and they both have a wicked protective streak running through them. "Have you ever seen him at one of the clubs?"

"No. I met him right before I graduated from school, and we only dated for a couple of weeks before I moved down to Spring City. But then he showed up there, dating my roommate. He didn't say anything, but it creeped me out."

"That's weird."

"That's what I said. Anyhow, she trashed my good props, not that I would've known how to explain them to my new boss, anyway."

"Well, Sunshine, do your little dance tonight, and hopefully we will conclude our business by the end of the year."

"All right. Thanks, Tony."

"See you later."

Because I've worked at all of his clubs, I've never gotten to know any of the other dancers. In the dressing room are a couple of women who are nice enough, recognizing me as what I am—a fill-in and not someone to bond with long term. We chat a little, and I learn they are all here because they didn't want to deal with the handsy drunkards guaranteed to push the boundaries at Rawhide tonight. Sometimes too much out-of-town money is a bad thing.

A blonde named Carrie points to a makeup counter. "You can use that station tonight."

"Thanks."

"Tony says you do burlesque."

"Yeah."

"I'll be interested in catching your show."

"Tonight's my last night, so I better make them good."

"Are you retiring? You're so young."

"Yeah, well, I want to work with kids, so you know how that goes."

"Oh yeah. Parts of the country won't even let drag queens read to kids, so they're definitely not going to let an exotic dancer teach them, even though one has nothing to do with the other."

"Exactly."

I focus on doing my makeup and applying false eyelashes. My face is damn near unrecognizable with all the color and thick black liner. Then I clip in rainbow hair extensions before styling my long locks into ponytails. I have a Rainbow Brite/Sailor Moon cosplay thing going on, and I used to have giant rainbow feather fans as part of my dance props. Of course, I left those behind and my roommate trashed them, so tonight I will do my ball, hula hoop, and pole routine four times and then call it a night. I don't care if one person watches me, much less tips me. I just need to fill in time between the real dancers and then go home to Rylie and Nyla.

Maybe I could practice my juggling on stage? As long

as I strip down to pasties and a g-string, I doubt anyone would care.

"Rainbow, you're on in fifteen minutes." Someone says above the din of female chatter.

The crowd is fairly sparse at eight pm. So I do my dance and then hang out backstage, playing on my phone. I text Rylie to see how his night is going.

Hey you. How are Nammy and Pappa?

Good. They asked Nyla to stay the night tonight, so I have my evening free.

Oh? Damn. I wish I were there. What are you doing?

They lifted our curfew and we have Mondays and Tuesdays off again, so two of the guys are taking their friend out for her birthday and invited me to dinner. After that, probably a drink at a club. Are you having fun with your girlfriends?

Ummm, ya know. We're getting the job done. I should be home by midnight.

I'll be waiting.

Will you?

Well, I might be asleep.

I could wake you up if you like.

I'd like to wake up with you in my arms again.

<3 I'd like that too.

Sounds like we have a plan. Our steaks are being served. I'll see you tonight?

Yes. Have fun and I'll see you soon.

Oh my god, I could have a night alone with Rylie and instead, I'm stuck here. Dammit. Two more hours, three more dances, and then I'm in Rylie's arms.

A little more than an hour later, a sweet, tiny, chatty thing with huge boobs comes back with Carrie to meet some of the other dancers. They talk about their lives outside of the club, their families, and why they do what they do. Since I'm not a career dancer, I mostly stay out of the conversation and hide in my corner, waiting until it's my turn to dance again.

Tony raps his knuckles on the doorframe and pokes his head in. "I'm back for the next hour, if you need me. Carrie, you're up next."

Carrie does her dance and then it is my turn, the club filling up in the last two hours. This is one of the hottest strip joints in town, so even on a Monday night, the crowds pick up around eleven. The lights on the stage are bright and the rest are dim, which I prefer. I'd rather not make eye contact if I can avoid it. Only at the end of the stage is it bright enough to see the crowd, and I rarely approach it.

My music plays overhead and I come out in a long wrap-around skirt with high slits on the sides and a butterfly-sleeved blouse tied between my breasts. I spin my hoop over my head, using it and the pole to do my dance. By the end of the first song I have my blouse off with my bikini top firmly in place, and I've removed my skirt, a pair of high-cheek boy shorts remaining.

A large figure moves through the shadows to stand at the end of the stage. I turn my back to ignore him, as I do all patrons, but then over the din and the music I hear Rylie's voice.

"You lied."

Chapter 7

Rylie

We end up at Diamonds and Pearls Cabaret, a birthday treat for Jepson and Jaxson's girlfriend, who has never been to a strip club before. I plan to give it another fifteen minutes—if that—and then I'll find a ride home. Honestly, I think I need to grab my own ride home regardless, as I suspect Jepson and Jaxson plan to give Maryanne more surprises in the back of the car behind the privacy glass.

Rex and I can share a car back to Spring City if he's willing to leave soon.

A new dancer comes on stage, but she's not like the other dancers. She's doing a burlesque-style routine with a hoop and a ball, almost like a sexy carnival performer. Her body is toned and muscular, unlike some of the skinny dancers, and although her rainbow hair keeps me from focusing on her face, her curves are more my speed.

It's when she unwraps her long skirt and flashes her

thick rainbow garter tattooed thighs that all the blood rushes from my face.

"Fuck." I hiss, blinking hard to change the channel on the reality TV playing before me.

It can't be.

She… fuck, no.

Not Sunshine.

Anyone other than Sunshine.

Jepson, Jaxson, and Maryanne are walking out, muttering their goodbyes, but I don't register their words as I pull myself up on my feet and drag my broken and betrayed bones to the end of the catwalk. I stare at her through unblinking eyes until she comes close enough to hear my words, "You lied."

Sunshine's eyes bug out as her gaze lands on my face. She drops her hoop. "Rylie."

I shake my head and say again. "You lied to me."

"No." She jumps off the stage and grabs my arm. "It's not what it looks like."

Even though she's the one touching me, the bouncer is on me in seconds, hauling me away from her.

"No!" She pushes the security guy away and grabs my hand. "Please, come with me."

I'm too shocked to react, letting her pull me through the crowd into one of the private rooms. She pushes me forward and then shuts the door behind her. "Rylie. Rylie? Say something."

Shaking my head, I slump against the wall. "You fucking lied."

"I owe a debt. This was my last night dancing, I promise."

"Debt?" All the dirty little vices one can accumulate go through my head.

Is it drugs?

Dear God, please don't let it be drugs. But what else could it be?

A man pounds on the door. "Rainbow?"

Sunshine's eyes grow wide. "It's okay, Tony."

"Fuck that, I'm coming in." A big guy, maybe six foot four and two hundred and twenty pounds, barges in. His eyes are razor-sharp as he looks her over and then casts them my way. "What the fuck is going on?"

Sunshine shakes her head "It's just a misunderstanding."

"Yeah, but you don't do private rooms, so who is this guy? Is this the stalker you were telling me about?"

"Stalker?" I look at her. "Have you heard from that asshole?"

"No, Tony, this is my boss. I take care of his little girl."

Tony visibly relaxes, blowing out a deep breath and running his hand through his thinning hair. "Shit. Of all the strip clubs in Denver. What are the fucking odds?"

Glancing around the room, I grab a seat in an oversized chair. "You have two minutes to explain before I walk out the front door."

Sunshine rambles quickly. Panic-infused doubt makes her cheeks flush and her hands tremble. "I've been dancing for Tony since I was a sophomore in college.

Halfway through my senior year, my scholarship didn't come through, and I wasn't going to graduate without a private loan. Tony made me a deal, but when I moved to Spring City, I missed a couple of payments. Then I got the job with you, and it gave me the extra funds I needed to send him some money. But I was already behind, and he asked me for a favor—"

"How much?" I interrupt.

"What?" She furrows her brow.

"You owe money for school and nothing else? How much?" Drugs or gambling, I'm expecting tens of thousands of dollars. A house or medical expenses, hundreds of thousands.

But one semester of school?

Tony clears his throat. "After tonight, six grand."

"Before tonight?"

"Seventy-five."

"Fine." I pull out my phone. "I'll transfer the money to you now."

Sunshine shakes her head. "Why would you do that?"

"It doesn't matter why. It's done." I don't look at her. Staring into her soft brown eyes will break me, and I refuse to give her that power over me. "What's your email?"

"So, I owe you instead of Tony?"

"You don't owe me shit." I lace my tone with disgust even though all I feel is heartbreak.

This is my love life? Am I going to attract beautiful

women who lie as easily as they breathe until I'm laid out on my deathbed?

I don't understand.

I don't understand how I fell for it again. "If you want to take your clothes off and dance for money, do it honestly. Don't do it because of some debt, or whatever excuse you have to give yourself. Live your life."

Her lips part, and she takes a step back as if I had slapped her.

Tony sighs, "Go change and grab your shit, Sunshine. You're done for the night."

Tears slip down her cheeks as she walks out of the room, leaving me with the big guy who comes off more like a cop than he does a sleazy strip club owner. "Those were some pretty pious words from a guy sitting in the VIP section of my dance club."

"I don't have a problem with dancers. I have a problem with liars."

"I get that. And I'm not going to make excuses for Sunshine, but I've known her for a long time, and if she didn't tell you about this, it's because she didn't think it was going to come up. She thought this was behind her. You're angry right now, so I have only one thing I'm concerned about. Do I need to be worried about you unleashing your anger later?"

"Who are you?" I push up out of my chair, my phone still in my hand.

"An ex-vice cop who now co-owns and runs respectable gentlemen's clubs. You don't strike me as an abusive person, but you are a big guy, and Sunshine is like a daughter to me. She's the only dancer I've ever let run her business her way, and the only one I've loaned money to—so I'm going to challenge you."

"I'm fine. She's fine. I won't kick her out on her ass. What's your email?" I'm getting annoyed with this guy, although he seems decent enough. Really, I just want to get the hell out of here as quickly as possible. I want to go home, take a hot shower, and maybe have a drink—something I rarely do.

Tony rattles off his email and the transaction goes through without issue.

"Sorry for the disruption," I order a car and slide my phone into my pocket.

He nods, checking his phone when it beeps. "Give her a chance to explain, Rylie. She's a good girl."

"Doesn't matter who, what, when, or why. She lied. How can I believe a word that comes out of her mouth?"

"People lie for all kinds of reasons. Find out her reason." Tony holds the door open for me. At the end of the hall, Sunshine stands there with her bag on her shoulder. Her hair and makeup are still prepped for the stage, and honestly, I don't recognize her right now.

"Did you drive?" She asks, her voice barely above a whisper.

"No. We took a car."

"I can give you a ride home."

I shake my head, unsure about being stuck in a car with her for the next hour. "Rex is with me. I need to check what he wants to do."

"Please, Rylie. Don't walk away angry. Don't let your

feelings for me solidify into apathy. We have to talk about this."

Rex walks up at that moment. "Man, what's going on?"

"Are you ready to go?" I glance his way.

He shrugs, his eyes going to Sunshine and then coming back to me. "Sure."

"I can give you a ride back to Spring City if you are okay with driving in an old Sentra?" She flashes him a small smile.

He motions to me, leaving it as my decision.

"Dammit." I roll my eyes. "Let's go."

I remove Nyla's booster and put it in the trunk, commandeering the backseat and forcing Rex to sit next to her. Between the two of us, we are way too big for this car, and now I'm thinking if Sunshine drives Nyla around, I need her in something a bit more robust.

Shit. *If she continues to drive Nyla around.*

What the fuck am I going to do about her? About us?

Until thirty minutes ago, I was excited about tonight. I couldn't wait to get home to Sunshine and our first night of utter privacy. I had plans that would have kept us busy until the morning light.

Now?

Rex and Sunshine conduct idle chit chat I refuse to take part in. Rex is also from a small farming community in Nebraska and is only a year or two younger than me. They talk about music and movies for forty-five minutes until we pull into his neighborhood and she rolls to a stop in front of his condominium.

"Thanks for the ride." He gives me a look that says *I have one hundred questions and I will ask them on Wednesday.*

I wave him away. "See you later."

Taking his place in the front seat, I keep my head straight as she pulls from the curb, but I can feel her staring at me. "Am I fired?"

"I'm not sure."

"Tell me this. Are you angry about the dancing or because I didn't tell you about it?"

Shaking my head, I stare out the window as a bitter hint of jealousy coats my tongue. "Both. You should have told me you needed money. We could've avoided this entire situation with one simple conversation, but lying was easier for you, and that concerns me."

"It wasn't easier. I wanted to tell you, but I thought it was in my past. And then Tony asked me for one more night and offered me three times my normal pay—"

"When did he ask you?" I chance a look in her direction as all the color drains from her face. I already know the answer because she asked for the night off.

"Three weeks ago."

"At least you're not lying about that."

She sighs, hitting the button to open the neighborhood gate and then the garage. We enter the house in awkward silence. Sunshine leans her hip against the counter and pulls at the synthetic rainbow strands decorating her hair, her heavily painted eyes on me.

She doesn't look like her right now, and honestly, with the raw emotions swirling between us, she doesn't feel like her either. There's no sunshine warming me like usual when she's nearby.

I shake my head and turn away from her. "I'm going to bed."

"Rylie!" She lunges at me, her hands clutching my shirt, as she drops to her knees. "You're angry."

I nod, my teeth clenched. "Yes."

"Fine. You have every right to be, but don't go to bed mad. Take your frustrations out on me."

"What are you saying?"

She pulls on my belt buckle and unzips my slacks before I realize what she's doing.

I wrap my fingers around hers, stopping her from pulling out my cock, and shake my head. "No, Sunshine. Not like this."

She deflates, slumps down until her ass hits her heels, and hangs her head. "I'm sorry."

I pull her to her feet. "Take a shower. You don't look like you right now."

"That's the point. It's not me. It's never been me."

If I peer past the heavy eyeliner and false lashes, I see her warm brown eyes staring back and searching mine. Carefully, I swipe my thumb over her bottom lip, smearing her red lipstick. "Go wash this shit off. I'll meet you there in a minute."

A small gasp escapes her lips as her eyes search my face with a glimmer of hope. "Okay."

She turns from me and retreats to her bedroom, while a plethora of emotions run through me. I'm not angry, but hurt and fearful that if I let this go as a one-time thing—

which is what I desperately want to do—then she'll somehow make a fool of me again in the future.

How do I make sure she feels safe enough to always come to me regardless of the problem? After the things I've been through, I need one hundred percent transparency in my relationships.

I run up to my bedroom and kick off my shoes, changing out of my slacks and button down and into a pair of loose joggers before coming back into the kitchen to make myself a whiskey and Sunshine a vodka tonic.

I slam back my drink, the liquid heat coursing through my veins and swirling in my stomach, but it calms my nerves and puts everything into crystal-clear focus. If I hadn't been so shocked tonight, I would've been mesmerized by the vision on the stage. Her athleticism, muscular form, and tantalizingly subtle tease are a work of art.

Of course, I hate the idea of anybody else ever seeing her like that, even though I have no right to claim her. Not yet anyway.

Pouring myself a second drink, I carry both into her bathroom, setting them on the counter next to her fluffy yellow towels. Leaning my ass against the counter with my eyes glued onto her slightly obscured naked form behind the frosted panes of her glass shower door, I cross my arms to keep from reaching out for her. My body responds to the memory of holding her luscious curves all night, and my decision becomes clear.

I need her.

I care for her.

I want her to be mine.

I've been falling in love with her from the moment we met, which means this situation needs to be dealt with, forgiven, and then left in the past so we can build a future together.

Sunshine finishes rinsing her hair, a surprised *eep* escaping her lips when she looks at me.

"You scared me. I thought you were joining me?"

Shaking my head, I grab one of her towels and hold it out for her. "I'm waiting for you to be you again."

She turns off the water and slides open the door. This is the first time I've seen her fully nude, and the desire to drop to my knees is stronger than I expect. Unapologetically, I let my gaze travel over her body. "There she is—my beautiful Sunshine."

"You hated seeing me like that."

"Not really. I hated everyone else seeing you like that."

"A tinge of possessiveness?" She raises her brow. "That's a good thing, right?"

I wrap the towel around her shoulders and gather up her wet hair, wringing out the excess moisture. Her nipples pebble in the cool air, so I take a step forward, pressing my warm body against hers. She tentatively wraps her arms around my waist and lifts her head, resting her chin against my sternum. "I'm sorry about tonight, Rylie."

I sigh, focusing on her hair. "Do you have any other secrets you need to tell me before we leave this night in the past?"

"Nothing that I consider a secret. Nyla asked if she could call me mommy on Saturday, but I told her it wasn't a good idea while I was still her teacher. Thankfully, she agreed."

"Yeah, she's going through something right now. Anything else?"

"I know this isn't an excuse, but I thought dancing for Tony was in my past, and considering everything I know about your ex, the last thing I wanted to do was give you something that would remind you of her when looking at me."

"We can talk about it more at another time if we have to. You should know, I'm not a grudge fuck kind of guy. I will never touch you out of anger. I'm way too big to mess around with stuff like that." I lean down and kiss her forehead and the tip of her nose before gently claiming her lips. "Besides, I would prefer our first time to be more of an exploration, which in my mind equals finesse."

She tenderly trails her fingertips over my pecs, teasing my nipples before sliding her hands over the bulge in my pants. "I like the idea of exploring each other."

I suck in my breath and arch into her hand. "We have until the morning light."

She smiles. "Let's get started."

Chapter 8

Sunshine

Rylie tosses my towel over the shower door and then lifts me in his arms, carrying me into my bedroom. He lays me down gently and glides his hands over my thighs. "You are really beautiful, Sunshine—outside as well as in."

I hope he means every word because, despite tonight's setback, I'm irrevocably in love with him. There's nothing like thinking I lost him to solidify my feelings. My heart broke when I saw him at the end of that catwalk, and I would have done anything to get him to not shut me out.

Anything.

Rylie stretches out beside me, one hand propping up his head, his eyes following the other as he languidly caresses my body. His teasing touch makes me crazy, but when I reach for him, he stops me, pulling my hands above my head. "Not yet. You don't get to touch me yet, Sunshine."

"When?" I moan as he lowers his mouth to my breast and sucks my nipple between his teeth. He applies a bit of pressure, just enough to sting, which causes me to arch my back off the mattress.

He chuckles, sliding his hand between my thighs that I spread wantonly for him. God, it feels like I've been waiting my whole life for this man to touch me. I'd take him any way he wants me. Hard and fast against the kitchen island. On my knees worshiping him and his cock. Slow and tender in the privacy of my bedroom like we are now. What I didn't expect was to be nearly out of my mind with need as Rylie takes his time torturing me.

"You can touch me when I'm done teasing you. Should I ask you to fuck your vibrator for me or get you off with my tongue? Or both?"

"You like to tease." I gasp as he slips his fingers between my slick folds, finding my throbbing clit with ease.

"It's been a long time for me. I want to enjoy myself and memorize every inch of you."

A small fragment of unease surges through my heart. "Is this a one time thing?"

He claims my lips at the same time he plunges his fingers inside of me, pumping his fingertips in rhythm with his tongue against mine. "I hope not."

Oh thank god.

His tongue tangles with mine, his fingers expertly stroking my G-spot as his thumb circles my clit.

"So hot and slick and perfect." He murmurs, pressing kisses to my neck, collarbone, and breasts.

"Rylie, I need to touch you."

"Put your fingers in my hair, Sunshine. Ride my face while I fuck you with my tongue."

"Oh, you have a filthy mouth." I muse. "I love it."

He smiles as he positions himself between my thighs. "I've had a PG filter on for so long, it takes me a while to get warmed up. But yes, I can be absolutely X-rated when appropriate."

"And I worried my subtle flirting had been lost on you." I tease, sliding my fingers through his thick hair.

His beard scratches my inner thighs most deliciously as he waggles his brow at me. "Not lost, although occasionally I wondered if you were doing it on purpose or not."

"Even when it wasn't on purpose, it was on purpose."

"Hmmm." He keeps his eyes on me as he sticks his tongue out, licking me from one end to the other. My pussy clenches and my eyes roll back as a moan escapes my lips. "I want you to come all over my mouth, Sunshine, and then all over my cock."

"Oh, I love hearing you talking like that."

And then there is no more talking as Rylie pushes my thighs wide with his massive shoulders and spears my wanton hole with his talented tongue. He laps at me, licking and sucking my clit into his mouth. I writhe against his lips, fisting his hair as my climax builds and he pushes me over the edge.

"Mmmm." He waits for my legs to stop shaking and then stretches out beside me again, his big hand splayed over my lower belly. "I like the way you come, Sunshine."

"Now it's my turn to make you come." I interlace my fingers with his and roll to my side to face him.

"Actually, I had a thought..." He rolls off the bed wearing his joggers and pulls me to my feet. "We will so rarely have the house to ourselves, free to walk around naked, so the last thing we should do is resign ourselves to your or my bedroom. Most of our moments will be stolen, so tonight we need to act out a few fantasies while we have the freedom to do so."

"Oh? Have you fantasized about me?" I slide my hand over his hard, erect cock, desperate to get my lips around him.

"You know I have." He lifts my hand to his mouth, kissing each fingertip.

"I've had a few fantasies myself."

"Like what?"

"Like riding you on your weight bench, so every time you lift, you think of me."

He walks me into the living room and pulls out a chair from the dining table. "You do that and I'm going to get hard every time I lift at the training facility."

"Is it worth it?" I tease.

He chuckles and sits down, pulling me between his splayed thighs. "The guys might get pissed, but I don't care."

"What are we doing, baby?" This is the first time I've called him baby out loud, but in my head, I've said it a million times.

"You are going to dance for me."

I shake my head. "I don't do lap dances or private

rooms. Never have. Honestly, I probably give horrible lap dances."

"Why don't you let me be the judge of that?" He pulls down his joggers, his beautiful cock large and hard and standing up so pretty in welcome for me. "I want you to ride me, Sunshine. Fuck me. Grind your pussy on my cock until you explode and soak me with your cum."

"How can I resist such a wonderful invite?" I smile, rotating my hips to the music in my head.

As if he realizes the problem at the same moment, he chuckles. "Guess I should have put on some music, huh? Alexa, play me Fever by Peggy Lee."

The song I was dancing to when he busted me tonight. This man will never cease to amaze me.

I drop to my knees between his splayed thighs, trailing my tongue up his exposed flesh. I'm desperate to have this man in my mouth, but if teasing is what he wants, teasing is what he gets. Standing flat-footed, I bend low at my waist and take him deep in my mouth, swirling my tongue over the head of his beautiful cock.

Rylie groans, his hand sliding into my hair.

"Nuh uh, huh." I pull out of his reach. "You don't get to touch me, remember? Right now, you are mine to torture, tease, and derive pleasure from."

"Then seek your pleasure, woman." His eyes narrow, but the look on his face is pure glee. He likes the prolonged tease, which we've had going between us for a month.

I turn around, wagging my ass in his face before

sitting down on his lap and reaching between my legs to grasp hold of his impressive cock. I hope I can take it all.

I mean, I will, but I hope it doesn't hurt.

I slide the head back and forth through my arousal, my pussy primed to take him deep.

"Oh, fuck me, Sunshine. Please."

"I plan to, baby." I turn around and straddle his lap, sinking down on him in one glorious move. Both of us moan, our eyes rolling back.

I wrap my arms around his neck, my toes barely touching the floor as I take a moment to adjust to his size and girth. "Baby, you have a lot to take in."

"But you take me so well."

"Like I was built for you."

"You were. I knew it the moment I met you." He wraps his big hands around my hips. "Ride me. Fuck me. Take me hard."

I wrap my legs and arms around him, gyrating my hips and grinding my pussy against him. He slides his hand between us, pressing his finger against my clit. It takes seconds before I explode and scream his name. "Oh Rylie."

He wraps his arms around me, pulling me tight against him. Burying his mouth into my neck, he grunts words I'm not sure he means for me to hear as he releases his orgasm deep inside me. "I love this, Sunshine. I love you."

My heart soars with his proclamation, but I'm afraid he didn't mean it, considering the night we had—the emotional rollercoaster we've been on. Had he said it last night, I would absolutely believe him and say it back.

Sucking in my breath, I pull back as both of us still and look him deep into his eyes. I don't want to embarrass him or risk him taking it back, so I just give him a small smile and kiss his lips gently. "You are amazing. I will never get enough of you."

He seems to understand what I mean without me having to say the words. With me wrapped around him, he stands as if I weigh nothing, and carries me into the kitchen, sitting me on the counter before pulling out. Grabbing a clean kitchen towel out of the drawer, he cleans us up. "I should've asked before we started, but are you on anything?"

"Yeah, I'm covered."

"Good, because I'm going to want to cum in you a lot."

"Sounds like the perfect end to every day to me."

Rylie cups my face and kisses me passionately. "It really does. You said you've fantasized about me fucking you. Anywhere in particular?"

I waggle my brows. "Right here against this very counter. Every time I do the dishes, I think about having you come up behind me, slide your hands around my hips, press your hard, aching cock into my back, and whisper in my ear how badly you want to bend me over."

"Naughty girl. Now, every time I see you doing the dishes, I'm going to be thinking the same thing."

"Don't be surprised if you catch me doing them every time you come home."

He pulls me off the counter and spins me around, his fingers wrapping around my hips. "Like this?"

I arch my back. "Perfect."

"Would it be weird if I brought you a frilly little apron?" He hisses into my ear as he grinds his cock into my ass.

"It would be weird if you didn't." I glance back over my shoulder.

"How flexible are you?" He lifts my knee, so it's on the counter. He has me spread wide as he slides the head of his cock along my slick opening.

"As flexible as you need me to be." I moan as he slips inside me, pumping his hips to fill me deep.

He steadies me with one hand on my thigh, pinning my leg up on the counter, the other cupping my breast as he pulls me back flush with his chest. The friction of him thrusting in and out of my pussy in smooth strokes has my mind drowning in pleasure.

"Oh god, Rylie. You feel so good."

"My little ray of sunshine. Do you want to come again?" He slides his fingertip over my clit.

"Yes." I whimper as my pussy clamps down on him. He groans, pulling my leg down and bending me over at the waist, pushing my breasts flat against the cold granite countertop.

"Brace yourself, baby." He wraps my long hair around his fist and digs his fingers into my hip as he pounds into me from behind, chasing his own orgasm. I love having him tender, but this is a next-level turn-on. I want Rylie to feel comfortable using his strength with me.

Own me, bend me, break me.

I'm his to use, pleasure, and love as he sees fit. I will accept him every way he wants to give and take me—from this night until our last.

"Is this okay?" He grunts behind me.

"Yes, baby. Harder. Fuck me hard, Rylie."

"Fucking perfect for me in every way." He growls as we come together.

Chapter 9

Rylie

Baby Shark plays on my phone, alerting me to the early hour and warm body in my arms.

I lean over Sunshine and answer my cell. "Good morning, Princess."

"Hi, Daddy."

"Why are you calling me so early?"

Nyla giggles. "Daddy, it's almost eight."

"Shit." I sit up with a start. Without thinking, I shake the lush, naked form lying beside me. "Sunshine, wake up. You're late for school."

"Daddy? Why is Miss Sunshine sleeping with you?"

Sunshine seems to realize what I've done at the same time my little girl calls me on it because she looks back at me with wide eyes. "Uh... we stayed up late talking and fell asleep."

Shit. I hate lying, which means I try not to do it myself, but this is too mature of a topic for a not-yet-five-year-old. However, it's almost the truth without giving details, so maybe she'll forgive me.

"Am I not going to school today?" Nyla continues, thankfully.

"I thought we'd have a daddy-daughter day since the team changed their schedule back to Mondays and Tuesdays off."

Sunshine slips out of my bed, a sliver of morning light shining through my curtains and dancing across her smooth skin. She casts me a furtive glance that speaks volumes before running out of my room.

"Are you going to pick me up soon?"

"I can leave here in the next thirty minutes. Do we want waffles this morning?"

"Yay!"

"Cool. Why don't you give Nammy the phone?"

"Okay."

Gloria comes on, a teasing lilt to her tone. "Good morning, Rylie—" and then she whispers "—and Miss Sunshine."

I sigh. "Good morning, Gloria."

"Sleep well?"

A stupid grin spreads across my face. "Not really."

"Good for you." She chuckles. "See you in the next hour?"

"Yeah. Can I take you and Sam to breakfast?"

"That would be lovely."

"Okay. I'll see you soon." I hang up and slip out of bed, forgoing my pants and descending the stairs to find

Sunshine in her shower. I can't stop myself—I mean, she's late anyway—and step in behind her.

She smiles and shakes her head. "I can't believe I'm late for work."

"Can you call in sick?"

"I called in late."

"Do we have time to get dirty and then clean?" I grab the body gel and lather up her yellow pouf before gently scrubbing her body. Sunshine faces me, leaning back against the tile wall and bringing up her foot so that she's open for me. I love her fearlessness and desire to make herself accessible to my wants, needs, and desires. While I'm sliding the soapy sponge between her legs, she's reaching between our bodies and stroking my fully roused cock.

"We'll make time." She moans as I caress her. "I love your body, Rylie, and the way you move it against mine."

"You bring out something in me, Sunshine. I've never come so many times in one night in my life."

"Really?"

"Yeah." I close my eyes as she tightens her grip on my shaft. Tossing the pouf over my shoulder, I slide my forearms under her knees and lift her off the ground. She wraps her arms around my neck as I slide deep inside of her.

"I love how you can pick me up and move me around effortlessly." She whimpers as I pump my hips. "It's so sexy."

"How am I going to keep my hands off of you once

Nyla is home?" I bury my face in her neck, pumping faster and harder and chasing my release.

Her pussy clenches around me as she locks her ankles behind my back, her orgasm causing nonsensical words to rush from her lips. I follow seconds later, thankful Sunshine is on birth control. I foresee a lot of stolen moments that could be as short as a few minutes with Nyla in the house. How do I introduce a love interest to my five-year-old? Especially a love interest who lives in the house with us?

After we ride out our climaxes, I set her feet down on the tiled floor. She smiles up at me drunkenly. "We'll figure it out, baby."

"I guess we will."

For the next week, we live a normal existence, waiting until Nyla is asleep to crawl into each other's beds. The team plays and wins at home on Sunday, and Nyla invites a few of the player's kids to her birthday party. The funny part is, I'm not sure which ones have been invited.

On Tuesday, I'm arriving at Gymboree an hour early with two boxes full of decorations, a cake, and bags of presents. To my surprise, Heather is there waiting in the lobby.

"What are you doing here?" I say with a bit more bite than necessary.

"Mom let it slip that there was a birthday celebration. I don't blame you or Nyla for not inviting me." She presses her lips together. "I heard you have a girlfriend now."

My brow furrows and I shake my head. It's none of her business, and I refuse to have this conversation with her.

She smiles and casts her eyes to the ground. "I'm not here to fight, Rylie. Mom says Nyla adores her nanny and that the two of you are happy with life right now. That's all I want, and I'm sorry I couldn't be part of that happiness. I really wish things could have been different. That I could have been different. You two deserve the best, and I hope you get it."

Letting out a slow breath, I turn my attention to the Gymboree employee. "Here are the decorations for the four pm party for Nyla Reynolds."

"Yes, sir. I'll take care of it." She smiles and takes the boxes with no questions asked.

Turning to Heather, I shove my hands in my pockets. For a long time, coming face to face with her filled me with a flurry of emotion.

Anger.

Desperation.

Sadness.

But now I feel nothing. Nyla is going to be okay without Heather. It sucks, but she'll be fine because she's an amazing child who loves and is loved by all she meets.

"Why are you here?" I ask again.

Heather grabs a giant bag full of brightly colored

tissue paper. "I was hoping you would give this to Nyla. I think she'll like it. At least I hope so."

"Are you not staying?"

She shakes her head slowly. "She told mom she doesn't want me here, and honestly, I don't blame her. Besides, my ride is waiting for me. I'm moving, Rylie. To Vegas. So I won't be around anymore, not that I was anyway."

"You're leaving the state without saying goodbye to your child?" I don't know why, but this shocks me. It shouldn't, but it does.

"I think it's for the best. Maybe I can FaceTime her this weekend and wish her a happy birthday?"

Jesus, at this point, I'm not sure what the right answer is. Stay and force her presence on our daughter or leave without a word. I guess she's already left multiple times without a proper goodbye, so what's one more time? "I think, maybe, Nyla will call you when she wants to talk."

Tears well in her eyes, but she nods and blinks them away. "That's probably the best answer."

"Have a nice life, Heather. I hope you find what you are looking for."

I watch her walk out, praying I've made the right decision. It only takes a minute for calm to wash over me, and I know I have. Heather needs to find her way, and the constant fear she will pop in and disrupt Nyla's life lifts from my shoulders.

My phone rings, a new ringtone alerting me to Sunshine's contact.

"Hey," I say plainly, unsure who is listening.

"Hey, handsome." She purrs, letting me know she is semi-alone. "Are you at Gymboree?"

"I am. I have delivered the cake and decorations."

"Fantastic. I'm putting the birthday girl in the car now with three of her friends. We should be there in twenty minutes."

"See you soon, Sunshine."

"Love you too." She says absentmindedly before disconnecting the call—a flurry of little girls chattering away in the background.

I let those words fly out of my mouth in the heat of the moment last week, but this is the first time she's said them back to me. Did she mean them? I know I did, even if the moment was wrong. We'd been pseudo-fighting an hour earlier. I was balls deep and coming when I said it. She never brought it up, never responded, but let me know she heard with her own subtle response of *forever*.

With Heather, I was swept up in a lifestyle that quickly became a responsibility. With Sunshine, I fell in love with the way she cared for my little girl before I let myself have more. Now that I've held her in my arms, I'm never letting her go.

She needs to know that.

I grab presents and a cake out of my Jeep and bring them inside, walking aimlessly until I see all the Minion and football decorations. The employees grab the cake from me and show me where to stash the presents.

"Is it true that you're with the Rocky Mountain Rangers?" A teenage boy asks coyly, as if we're having a super secret conversation.

"Yeah." I chuckle.

"Man... uh, my boss would kill me if she knew I was asking, but can I get you to sign my jersey?"

"Yeah, man. There might be a few other players here too, if you want to wait."

"Really? Who?"

"Honestly, I have no idea."

"Man, you are the coolest. Thanks."

Glancing out the window, I catch Sunshine walking across the parking lot with four overly excited girls and rush to the front door to greet them.

"Daddy!" Nyla jumps into my arms.

"Happy Birthday, Princess."

"I have been waiting for this all day." She rolls her eyes dramatically.

"Good, I'm sure that you will be exhausted by the time we're done."

Nyla wraps her arms around my neck and whispers in my ear. "Did you tell Miss Sunshine you love her?"

I pull back and look her in the eye. "Why would you ask that?"

"Because I heard her say *I love you too* in the car."

I frown. "I don't exactly know how to answer that."

Nyla shrugs. "I love her, so you should, too."

"Is it that easy?"

"Yeah, Daddy, it's that easy. Can I go play?"

"Yes, but you have to greet your guests as they come in."

"Okay."

Sunshine flashes me a surreptitious smile. "Sorry about that. The words just came out."

"Did you mean them?"

"I've been saying them in my head for weeks, but I didn't want you to feel trapped by them."

"I said them to you last week."

"I wasn't sure if you meant them." She glances around and lowers her voice. "People say crazy shit when they come."

Moving to stand in front of her with my eyes on the girls playing in the jungle gym, I wrap my hand around Sunshine's hip. "Yeah, they do, but I meant it when I said *I love you.* Nyla will always be my priority, and I had resigned myself to never finding a woman because it wouldn't be fair to start a relationship with somebody and ask her to be second place on day one. But you took that role before you even walked into our house. If I loved nothing else about you, your selflessness had me hooked." I lower my mouth to her ear and flex my hand against her waist. "But then you had to be smart, sweet, beautiful, and so unbelievably fucking sexy. You're the total package, Sunshine, and the woman I want to spend the rest of my life with."

She sucks in her breath and looks me in the eye. "I'm not going anywhere, baby. Nyla is also my priority, and I love being a part of your lives."

I catch Nyla watching us from the top of the castle, a big smile on her face. Purposefully, I kiss Sunshine's cheek and throw my little girl a wink. She giggles, and I know we have her blessing.

This is it.

Day one of our lives as a family.

No more secrets, not even from Nyla, starting now.

From this day forward, it's the three of us and anyone else that comes along, but that's a conversation for another time.

Epilogue

Rylie - One Year Later...

"Will you be my girlfriend?"

Those are the first words I hear as I enter the house. My ears perk up and I swing my gaze to Sunshine who is busily making sandwiches, her lips pressed together as she suppresses her laughter.

"What the hell?"

I'm assuming Nyla is downstairs in her playroom, but I don't know who else is in the house.

Sunshine shakes her head. "Danny came over to play. He's got a crush."

"She's not allowed to have boyfriends." I say louder than necessary. I don't care if he's the heir to the Scott family fortune, the Rangers football team, or my star quarterback's son—stay away from my little girl.

Sunshine giggles as she cuts two sandwiches into squares, puts them on plates, and sets them on the table. She calls down to the brood below, four plates, I assume, means four children. "Snacks are ready."

After our championship season last year, Sunshine created a mommy crew with some of the girlfriends and wives where they trade-off playdates when we play out of town. For home games, the organization offered us a family room overlooking the stadium.

Kids run up the stairs, Nyla jumping into my arms as soon as she sees me. "Daddy! You're home."

"Hey, Princess. What are you wearing?" She's dressed up like a pirate. Actually, all the kids are.

"My Halloween costume. We're having a trunk-or-treat party this Wednesday."

Sunshine rests her hip on the counter and nods. "Family fun day at the Stadium. The kids wanted to be the lost boys from Hook."

A sinking feeling settles in my stomach. They tried to get me to dress up as Peter Pan last year, but thankfully the costume was too small and indecent for public consumption. This year, I doubt Sunshine got my measurements wrong.

"Oh, no." I shake my head.

She waggles her brows. "You are going to look so good in green tights."

"Please tell me I'm not the only one."

"Oh no. Amelia's on task to convince Declan to dress up too. As well as a few other players."

I let Nyla down so she can eat her snack with her friends, and pull Sunshine into my arms. Placing my lips near her ear, I smile as she shudders in my hands. "And how are you going to convince me?"

"I have plans to get you in and out of those tights."

"You better." I kiss her cheek and smack her ass before pulling away, aware of our audience. Nyla, who just turned six and is in the first grade, watches us with a big smile on her face.

"You want a sandwich, baby?" Sunshine returns to her lunch meat and loaf of bread. "Or a protein shake?"

"I'm good until dinner. Guess I'll go take a shower—" I wave up the stairs and mutter under my breath "—by myself." This is the first Sunday I've come home to a brood. Usually, by the time I get home Nyla is asleep, she's at someone else's house and Sunshine is waiting for me in something skimpy and easily accessible, or the house is empty because its the next morning and they are both at school. But we played the morning Sunday game in Denver today, so it's early and I'm betting everyone else is getting a little alone time before they pick up their kids.

Sunshine presses her lips together but gives me a look that speaks volumes.

Later.

Later.

Later.

We've been together for over a year, and although I've yet to pop the question, there is no doubt in our minds that we are a committed family. Sunshine now teaches kindergarten and is no longer a teacher's aide, so Nyla refers to her as mommy at home and at school. The simple term seems to give both of the women in my life immense joy, and whatever makes them happy makes me happy.

In our bedroom hangs a collage of black and white photos. Close-ups of my hand resting on Sunshine's thigh, her hand framing the tattoo of Nyla's name inked on my shoulder blade, my bearded face cradled by her bare neck, her glossy lips near my ear. Of course, under lock and key we have much racier photos for our private viewing pleasure.

Many hours later, Nyla is sleeping hard after a full day of hard play, and Sunshine is crawling into bed between my legs freshly showered. I offered to join her, but she told me she had other plans. She runs one hand up my inner thigh, and that's all it takes to send blood rushing to my cock.

"Hard day, babe?" I hiss as she pulls my cock free from my boxers.

"We both worked hard today, but I've been thinking about taking you in my mouth since you teased me before leaving for Denver yesterday." She licks me from base to tip, before wrapping her lips around me and taking me deep. My eyes roll back and I groan, giving myself over to her for as long as I can take it. I never let her finish me, unless I'm really tired, because I like to prolong my release as long as possible and make sure she comes at least twice to my every one.

It's almost a competition. My laid back, warm, sunshiny queen likes to tempt me into losing control. "Ah, damn. Your mouth feels good."

"Come for me, tonight." She turns her soft brown eyes up at me. "I want to taste you. Drink you down. Swallow every drop you have to give me."

Goddammit. I'm going to give in. I always give in. I slide my fingers into her hair and arch my hips, gently fucking her mouth, her fingers gripping me tightly. Within a minute my toes are curling and I'm coming hard, shooting my load down her throat.

Sunshine crawls up my body and rests her chin on my sternum, smiling up at me while batting her eyelashes. "I love you, Rylie."

"I love you too, Sunshine."

"I have something for you to think about..."

I narrow my eyes. "Why do I think you're softening me up for something?"

"I'm not. One has nothing to do with the other, but if you're feeling relaxed and generous right now, I have something I want."

I pull her up my body so her thighs are straddling my hips, my cock nestled against her hot, wet cunt. "Like I can deny you anything."

"This is for me and Nyla."

"Then the answer is definitely yes."

She smiles. "I want to give her a kitty cat for her birthday next week."

Frowning, I cup her face and swipe my thumb over her bottom lip. "That's it?"

"And maybe a puppy for Christmas, but first we'll test out having a kitten."

Chuckling, I shake my head and kiss her plump lips. "Baby, you're the one who will be home the most to train and care for whatever and whoever you bring into this house. If you want to take on the responsibility, I'm thrilled to chip in anyway I can."

"I just think a pet is the second best thing to a sibling and she would love it. One of the teachers had a litter six weeks ago and is getting ready to ween them."

"Can we go on Tuesday so I can come with you? I'd love to see her face when she meets all of them."

"Yes." She wraps her arms around me and squeezes. "Thank you."

"No, babe, thank you. Thank you for loving me and Nyla. For making our house a home with warmth and affection. Only because of you can we do and have things like this. I love you so damn much." I sigh, rolling her onto her side and pulling her knee up to my hip. "Shit, I wanted to wait and make this special, but I feel like now is the time."

"What's that?" Sunshine caresses my chest and trails her fingers over my arms.

I reach into my nightside table behind me and pull out a plain brown paper envelope. Rolling back to face her, I unfold the paper until a ring slides out.

The smile falls from Sunshine's face as I pick up the yellow diamond ring. "It's beautiful."

"This isn't a big romantic gesture, but that doesn't mean I haven't been thinking about this for the last year. I bought this ring a few months ago, not because I had something planned, but because when I saw it I immediately thought of you. The light yellow reminds me of warmth, love, and sunshine—which is who you have been for us since the day we met. You brought light and joy into my home, and I've loved you ever since that day. I have no intentions of ever letting you go, and whether we marry tomorrow at the court house or two years from now in the biggest church celebration ever held, you are mine and always will be."

I grab her hand and place the ring at the top of her finger. "Will you marry me?"

"Yes. Today, tomorrow, whenever. I don't need fancy things, I just need you and Nyla." She kisses me through her giggles. "However, Nyla really liked wearing her princess dress at Deacon's wedding, so I'm thinking she would not approve of us eloping."

I chuckle. "Agreed."

She lays her diamond clad hand flat against my chest and admires it like she has before whenever she gets that dreamy look in her eye, thinking about how great the vision would be captured on film, and I know what our next picture for our walls will be.

Coming Next: Devlin and Rex's story is Man to Man Coverage
Signed paperbacks and bundle discounts are available here.
Subscribe to the Witty, Wicked & Wild Community for early access and more.

Also by Kameron Claire

Want more **Witty** Tongues, **Wicked** Needs, & **Wild** Deeds?

Hollywood Lights (Pre-Order)

** Billionaire Romance **

Show Time (Securing Selyne)

Money Shot

Three Shot

Martini Shot

Long Shot

Veteran K9 Team

** Military Romance **

Mine to Cherish

Mine to Crave

Mine to Possess

Mine to Adore

Mine to Covet

Mine to Worship

Mine to Protect

Mine to Treasure

Hot Nights with the Boss

** Forbidden Office / Age-Gap Romances **

Dating the Boss

Flirting with the Boss

Teasing the Boss

Tempting the Boss

Rangers Football

** Sports Romance **

Play Action Fake

Quarterback Sneak

Personal Foul

Two-Point Conversion

Red Zone

Man to Man Coverage

Short Story Collections and Bundles

Animal Attraction 4-Story Collection

Vegas Nights 4-Story Collection

Last Stand Saloon 4-Story Collection

Instalove Bundle

About the Author

USA Today Bestselling Author Kameron Claire writes stories with witty tongues, wicked needs, and wild deeds. Her books emphasize strong female leads and the protective alpha males who know how to love and support kick-ass, take-charge women. Many of her books contain military veterans, boss babes, gentle but dominant men, and goofy K9 hijinks.

Find her everywhere via linktr.ee/kameronclaire
Signed Paperbacks and discounted eBook bundles are available exclusively on her store
Subscribe to the Witty, Wicked & Wild community and read all her books online for as little as $5 a month.

www.ingramcontent.com/pod-product-compliance
Lightning Source LLC
Chambersburg PA
CBHW030146010826
48973CB00002B/746
9781965090046